They were here—alone

And it was Christmas—which had nothing to do with anything, except that Rachel was suddenly tempted to give herself a gift she'd been wanting for years.

Somehow, Lucas's right hand slipped between them, closing gently around her left breast. Rachel caught her breath as shattering sensations coursed through her. Lucas pushed the lace cup of her bra out of the way, giving him better access to her sensitized nipple. She arched restlessly, her right knee bending, sliding up his leg.

"You used to slap my hand when I did this," Lucas said, circling his thumb in a way that made her gasp.

"Now I'll slap it if you stop," she murmured.

His husky chuckle was a sweet reward. Lucas's laughter was so rare these days. Suddenly his eyes darkened with an almost feral hunger and he rolled, pulling her beneath him on the hard stone floor. "I've dreamed about having you, here, like this," he muttered. "I've wanted you since the first time I saw you. I've never stopped wanting you."

Rachel reached up with both hands to pull his mouth down to hers. "I want you, too," she whispered. "Make love with me, Lucas."

Dear Reader,

I have always loved Christmas. The traditions, the music, the decorations, the food, the smells—and the special significance of the holiday—everything about the season appeals to me. When I finished the first three books of the Southern Scandals series, I knew I would have to bring Emily's long-lost brother home to clear his name. The McBride family simply wasn't complete without him. And what better time than Christmas for reunions and redemption?

The "scandalous" McBrides have become very special to me during this series and I hate to leave them. Maybe I'll visit them again someday. In the meantime, enjoy watching Lucas, the wildest of the McBrides, give the gossips of Honoria a Christmas they'll never forget.

Wishing you a season filled with joy and romance,

Gina Wilkins

P.S. For those of you who missed any of the previous books in the Southern Scandals trilogy, you can order #668 *Seducing Savannah,* #676 *Tempting Tara,* or #684 *Enticing Emily* from the Customer Service Center. See details below.

Don't miss any of our special offers. Write to us at the following address for information on our newest releases.

Harlequin Reader Service
U.S.: 3010 Walden Ave., P.O. Box 1325, Buffalo, NY 14269
Canadian: P.O. Box 609, Fort Erie, Ont. L2A 5X3

Gina Wilkins
THE REBEL'S RETURN

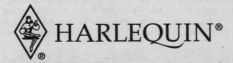

TORONTO • NEW YORK • LONDON
AMSTERDAM • PARIS • SYDNEY • HAMBURG
STOCKHOLM • ATHENS • TOKYO • MILAN • MADRID
PRAGUE • WARSAW • BUDAPEST • AUCKLAND

ISBN 0-373-25810-0

THE REBEL'S RETURN

Copyright © 1998 by Gina Wilkins.

This edition published by arrangement with Harlequin Books S.A.

® and TM are trademarks of the publisher. Trademarks indicated with ® are registered in the United States Patent and Trademark Office, the Canadian Trade Marks Office and in other countries.

Printed in U.S.A.

1

LUCAS MCBRIDE had spent the past fourteen Christmases alone. And he'd had every intention of spending this one the same way. But that was before a two-month-old article in the Honoria *Gazette* had brought him back to Honoria, Georgia, a town he'd once vowed never to set foot in again.

Strung with multicolored Christmas lights, even the oldest part of downtown Honoria looked festive. Enormous wreaths made of tinsel hung from each lamppost. As he drove down Main Street, deserted on this Sunday evening only five days before Christmas, Lucas looked behind the decorations to note that many of the twenties-era buildings were unoccupied, the windows boarded up or gapingly empty. The few remaining establishments looked as though they struggled to survive. A Revitalize Downtown poster fluttered halfheartedly on a pole beneath a glittering wreath.

He passed the corner of Main and Oak, where he and his teenage buddies used to hang out on Saturday nights, smoking cigarettes and trying not to look too anxious to meet the girls who cruised by in their daddies' cars. The alley behind the old, empty hardware store brought back memories of a fight Lucas and his pals had gotten into with a bunch of football jocks from rival Campbellville.

Chief Packer had broken up the melee and hauled all the participants to the city jail.

Lucas had spent that night in a cell. His father had been the only one who hadn't come to bail out his son.

It was the first night Lucas had spent in jail, but it hadn't been the last. Chief Packer had made arresting Lucas a hobby after that.

At the end of the block sat what had once been the old soda shop. Lucas had met Rachel Jennings there.

She'd been seventeen, he'd been nineteen. During the next ten months, they'd come to see themselves like Romeo and Juliet, kept apart by old family feuds. They'd met in secret, heightening the romantic thrill of their trysts. No one had been aware of their feelings for each other—until Rachel's brother Roger had found out about them.

Few of the townspeople would have imagined that the fiery-tempered bad boy, Lucas McBride, had a hidden streak of romanticism. But the events that had eventually run him out of town had destroyed whatever idealism he'd once possessed, just as time had decayed the buildings of old downtown Honoria.

Lucas had driven through the west part of town earlier, and had hardly recognized the heavily developed area with its shopping strips and fast-food restaurants and service stations and car-sales lots. He still remembered when his uncle Caleb had taken him deer hunting in the woods that had once stood there.

Progress, he thought, looking at the sadly dignified brick building that had once held the old five-and-dime store, wasn't all it cracked up to be.

Seeing the changes in his former hometown inevitably made him think of what else had changed since he'd left in the middle of that spring night so long ago. His father was dead now. His cousins scattered. His baby sister a grown woman. And Rachel...

As always, he pushed back his thoughts of Rachel into the darkest part of his mind, along with the other painful memories of his past. At least he wouldn't have to face her on this reluctant visit. He knew she'd moved away from Honoria not long after he had.

Out of old, half-forgotten habit, he turned right on Maple Street, thinking he'd drive past the high school and see if that had changed as much as everything else. Almost immediately, he saw a flashing blue light reflected in his rearview mirror. The dark-colored Jeep had pulled out of nowhere and was now right on Lucas's rear bumper, the light flashing from its dash identifying it as a police officer's vehicle.

Hell. Lucas had been back in Honoria less than two hours and already he was being hassled by the local authorities.

Apparently, some things hadn't changed at all.

He drove into the deserted parking lot of an auto-repair shop and stopped beneath a street lamp decorated with a glowing, horn-blowing Christmas angel. He rolled down the driver's side window and pulled his wallet out of the back pocket of his jeans, extracting his driver's license from its plastic sleeve. He'd been through this drill enough to know what to do.

The thirty-something officer was dressed in civies—a heavy denim jacket over a plaid flannel shirt and jeans. He held a badge in his hand to identify himself.

"License and registration, please," he said in a low drawl that marked him as a native Southerner.

Lucas held the license out the open window. "What did I do?"

"Did you happen to notice that you turned the wrong way on a one-way street?" the officer asked dryly as he pulled a penlight out of his pocket and aimed it at the driver's license.

"Maple's one way now? Hell, I didn't notice." Lucas glanced automatically toward the street, wincing when he saw the prominently displayed one-way arrow at the exit of the parking lot.

The officer looked at the license in his hand, then seemed to go very still. His voice held a note of strain when he asked, "You're Lucas McBride?"

Lucas knew this guy hadn't been around fifteen years ago. Did they instruct all new cops to be on alert for Lucas McBride, in the unlikely event that he ever reappeared?

"Yeah, I'm McBride. What of it?"

The officer sighed. "I can't give you a ticket tonight."

Startled, Lucas scowled suspiciously. "Why not?"

"I'm marrying your sister in a couple of weeks."

Lucas's hands went slack on the steering wheel. "Well, hell."

The officer tossed the driver's license back through the window.

"That's about the size of it," he muttered. And he didn't sound any happier about the situation than Lucas was.

LUCAS DREW a deep breath as he stared at the house in which he'd spent the first twenty years of his life. Though multicolored Christmas lights glowed from the eaves, and porch lights burned on either side of the front door, the night's darkness wrapped around the place like a heavy blanket that might have seemed cozy to some, but had ultimately felt smothering to Lucas.

"It looks the same as I remember it."

Wade Davenport nodded. "It needs some maintenance. I'll be taking care of that when I move in."

"You and Emily are going to live here when you're married?"

"Yes."

His gaze still focused darkly on that white-frame, black-shuttered house with its wraparound porch and winter-browned lawn, Lucas muttered, "Are you sure that's such a good idea? No marriage has ever lasted long in this house."

"We intend to change that."

Lucas had a sudden urge to climb back in his car and speed away, as fast as he'd driven when he'd made his escape fifteen years earlier. He'd made a mistake coming back here. Emily was obviously safe and well, busy with her own plans. She was marrying a cop, going on with her life. She probably hadn't given her long-lost half brother more than a passing thought in years.

He'd been a fool to let a strange compulsion draw him back here—a vague, unsettling feeling that Emily was in trouble, that she needed him. It was obvious that he'd been wrong.

He took a step back toward his car. "It's too late for an unannounced visit. Tell Emily I'll give her a call sometime, okay?"

"If I let you leave now, she'd never forgive me." Wade's voice was even, but there was a faint hint of steel beneath the easy drawl. "I think it'd be better if we just go on in."

Lucas narrowed his eyes. Davenport had insisted on following Lucas to the old homestead after he'd stopped him on Maple Street. "Why are you so determined for me to see her tonight?"

"Because I want to be there when you talk to her." Wade crossed his arms over his solid chest and leveled a look at Lucas, his brown eyes glittering in the gleam of security lighting, his face shadowed.

Lucas lifted an eyebrow. "You don't trust me?"

Wade shrugged.

Running a hand through his hair, Lucas released a deep breath. "I suppose you've heard about me."

"A few things."

"None of them particularly flattering, I'm sure."

"Let's just say no one's suggested naming a street after you."

A dry chuckle escaped him. "Can't see that ever happening around here."

Davenport motioned toward the house. "After you."

Glaring, Lucas took a reluctant step forward. "Never did like cops," he muttered.

"From what I've heard, the feeling's been mutual," Wade replied dryly.

Ringing Emily's doorbell was one of the hardest things Lucas had done in fifteen years. Well aware of the cop hovering behind him, Lucas wished himself any place but here, still cursing himself for giving in to the impulse to return home.

Emily had been eleven years old the last time he'd seen her. He'd been twenty. She probably wouldn't recognize the thirty-five-year-old man on her doorstep. And she had no reason to welcome him back into her life.

He'd left without even telling her goodbye.

The door opened. The young woman who stood framed in the doorway had curly, golden-blond hair, big blue eyes and fair skin lightly dusted across the nose with faint, gold freckles.

Though time had wrought its changes in her, Lucas would have known her anywhere.

She'd become a beautiful young woman. And it made him ache to look at her and think of all the years of her life he'd missed.

It had been his choice to leave. Given the same circumstances, he knew he would do the same thing again. But that didn't mean he had no regrets.

The smile of welcome she'd worn for her fiancé faded when she saw Lucas. Her forehead creased with a puzzled frown. "Wade? Is this a friend of yours?"

Lucas stepped more fully into the light. "Hello, Emily."

She studied him another moment, then stiffened. "Oh, my God," she whispered. "Lucas?"

He nodded, rather surprised that she'd identified him so quickly. She'd been just a little girl....

Prepared for anger, antagonism, or worse, indifference, Lucas was caught totally off guard when she threw herself against him, her arms in a stranglehold around his neck. "I can't believe you're here," she whispered into his ear.

His arms closed automatically around her. His mind went temporarily blank. Of all the scenarios he'd imagined when Emily first saw him, this hadn't been one of them.

He felt his throat tighten. It had been a long time since he'd been hugged so warmly. Since he'd been hugged at all, for that matter. And, damn...it felt pretty good.

"I take it you're glad to see him?"

Wade's dry question made Emily finally draw back. She released Lucas and turned to give her fiancé an equally fervent hug. "You found my brother for me. Oh, Wade, thank you. What a wonderful Christmas present."

Wade gave Lucas a rueful look over her head. "As much as I'd like to claim credit for making you this happy, I'm afraid I can't. I had nothing to do with your brother showing up."

Emily pulled back to look questioningly from Wade to Lucas and back again. "Oh. I just assumed—"

Wade draped an arm over her shoulders. "Let's go inside and talk about it. It's too cold for you to be out here without a jacket."

"Yes, of course. Come in, both of you."

She reached to take Lucas's hand, pulling him

inside as if she was afraid he'd take off if she let go. "Oh, Lucas, it's so good to have you home."

Home. The word made him frown again as he stepped over the threshold. This hadn't been his home for a very long time.

Funny how little had changed, though, he thought as he looked around the living room. The couch and chairs were new since he was here last, but the wooden tables and the old sideboard covered with photographs had been here as long as he could remember. A fresh-cut fir, almost sagging beneath the weight of the many ornaments hanging from its branches, stood in the big window, the same place they'd always put their Christmas trees.

"So you and Lucas just happened to arrive at the same time?" Emily asked Wade.

Wade chuckled. "Actually, he and I met on Maple Street. He thought he could get away with driving the wrong way on a one-way street."

Emily laughed. "Maple was made one-way five or six years ago, Lucas."

"Yes, I know that now." He turned to face his sister, studying the changes in her. "You look... great," he said lamely, shoving his hands in the pockets of his jeans in an awkward gesture that mirrored his discomfort.

She beamed at him, her face still flushed with excitement. "Thank you. You look exactly the same as I remember you."

Time had obviously played tricks with Emily's memory. Lucas was well aware that he bore little resemblance to the skinny twenty-year-old he'd once been.

Emily had just started to speak again when they were suddenly interrupted by a child's voice. "Daddy! Miss Em—er—Mom and me had hot fudge sundaes for dessert. With whipped cream and cherries on top!"

A snub-nosed boy with flame-red hair wrapped his arms around Wade's waist. "And we watched *Rudolph the Red-Nosed Reindeer* and *Frosty the Snowman*. Who's that?"

Since the question was asked without a pause for breath, it took the adults a beat to catch up.

Emily spoke first. "This is my brother, Lucas McBride. Lucas, this is Clay Davenport."

Looked as though Lucas's little sister was about to become a stepmom. Lucas was finding it hard to adjust to so many changes at once. "Nice to meet you, Clay."

The boy studied him curiously. "You're her brother?"

"Yes." Lucas saw no reason to explain that he and Emily shared the same father, but different mothers, making them half siblings.

"She told me she had a brother, but she hasn't seen you in a long time. Where've you been?" the boy asked with the simple directness of childhood.

Lucas felt the corners of his mouth twitch with a slight smile. "Here and there."

"Does this mean you're my uncle?"

Lucas was struck by the question. He'd never been anyone's uncle before. "I suppose I will be, after my sister and your dad are married."

"Cool. I'm getting a new bike for Christmas."

That easily, the boy had accepted Lucas's presence.

Wade chuckled and ruffled his son's red hair. "Being kinda' cocky there, aren't you, boy? You've only asked Santa for a new bike. You haven't actually gotten one, yet."

Clay didn't look particularly concerned.

Emily hit the side of her head. "What am I thinking, leaving everyone standing this way? Please, sit down. Can I get you anything? Coffee? Iced tea?"

Lucas didn't particularly want anything, but he needed a few moments to recover from this unexpectedly enthusiastic reunion. "Iced tea sounds good."

Wade also asked for tea.

Wade settled onto the sofa and nodded toward the two chairs grouped nearby. "Have a seat."

It was more of an order than an invitation. Lucas thought it was pretty obvious Wade Davenport wasn't overjoyed that his future brother-in-law had reappeared.

Lucas couldn't really blame the guy. Davenport had probably heard talk around town about the infamous Lucas McBride, generally believed to have literally gotten away with murder.

Having little experience making polite conversation with cops—and no experience with future brothers-in-law—Lucas didn't know quite what to say to fill the taut silence. "I, er, was sort of surprised that Emily recognized me. After all these years, I'd half expected her to have forgotten me."

"She's never forgotten you. Never stopped wondering why you left without telling her goodbye."

"I had my reasons," Lucas said coolly, keeping in mind that young Clay was watching them curiously.

"I'm sure you did. Just as I'm sure you have a reason for coming back."

Lucas's only answer was a shrug. He wasn't ready to lay all his cards on the table just yet.

Emily came back into the room, balancing a loaded tray carefully. Wade sprang to his feet to take it from her. He set it on the coffee table, careful not to spill the three glasses of iced tea or the small glass of milk. Emily distributed the drinks, then handed Lucas a plate of what appeared to be sliced banana-nut bread.

"I thought you might like to have a slice of this," she explained to Lucas with an endearingly shy smile. "Aunt Bobbie brought it over earlier today. I remember that you always loved her banana-nut bread."

Lucas was startled all over again. "You remember that?"

"Yes. And so does Aunt Bobbie. She mentioned it when she came by earlier. She and I both wished you were here to enjoy it with us. And now you are." Emily blinked several times, her eyes looking unnaturally bright.

Lucas sincerely hoped she wasn't going to cry. "How is Bobbie?" he asked quickly, to distract her.

Emily smiled again as she sat beside Wade and Clay on the couch. "She and Uncle Caleb are both fine. Their family is growing. Tara and Trevor are both married now, and Trevor has a two-year-old son. Trent's a senior at the Air Force Academy."

The cousins she'd named were all considerably younger than Lucas, closer to Emily's age. He hardly remembered them, but he feigned interest. He swallowed a bit of banana-nut bread, which tasted every bit as good as remembered. "Sounds like they're all doing okay."

"Yes. And Savannah's married now, too. Her twins are almost fourteen now."

Lucas didn't have to feign his reaction that time. "Fourteen? Savannah's not much older than you."

"She had them when she was seventeen. It's a long story. I'll tell you about it later. She and her family live in Campbellville. Aunt Ernestine lives with them."

Lucas winced. He remembered Ernestine. His father's sister-in-law had always been a difficult woman. She'd given Lucas a few scathing lectures about his responsibility to the family name. As if the McBride name had been all that sterling even before Lucas had done his part to tarnish it.

Emily's expression turned suddenly serious. "You haven't asked about Dad. Do you know he died last spring?"

Lucas nodded. "I know."

"He was sick for a long time. The last couple of years he was totally bedridden. He couldn't even speak."

Wade covered Emily's hand with his. "Emily took care of your father during his illness, with very little outside help. And with very little thanks, from what I understand."

Lucas gazed into his glass. "I can't imagine my father thanking anyone for anything, unless he changed considerably after I left."

"He never changed," Emily said with a touch of wistfulness.

"Did you…" Lucas hesitated, not knowing quite how to ask the question that had haunted him for so long. "Was everything okay for you here—after I left, I mean?"

"I was never mistreated, if that's what you're asking. Dad made sure I was fed and healthy, that my homework was done and my teeth were brushed. Aunt Bobbie took pains to see that my clothes were in style and that I stayed involved in youth groups and school organizations, so I would have plenty of friends. After Grandmother Mc-Bride died, Aunt Bobbie went out of her way to serve as a mother figure for me."

"So you were happy." He thought maybe he could let go of some of the guilt he'd been carrying around about the way he'd deserted his little sister.

A jumble of emotions crossed Emily's face, bringing the guilt back in full force. "I suppose so," she said, though her tone wasn't particularly convincing. And then she smiled and squeezed Wade's hand. "I'm very happy now."

Lucas thought of the article he'd read, the one that had brought him back to Honoria. Emily had been attacked right here in her home, when she'd interrupted an apparent robbery. The only item listed that had been stolen from her was something that Lucas had thought long buried.

Again, he wasn't quite ready to talk about that yet. Especially not with Wade Davenport and his kid listening. And, apparently, Emily had fully recovered from the attack. She looked healthy and happy. "I'm glad to hear it."

Emily's expression turned suddenly pensive again. "Dad was very angry with you after you left. I suppose you knew he would be."

Lucas nodded.

"He didn't leave much of an estate," Emily continued. "The medical bills wiped out most of the cash. Dad had some life insurance, but it wasn't an enormous amount. He left the house to me. I sold it to Wade."

Lucas lifted an eye brow as he looked at Wade, who was listening without expression. "You bought the house?"

Wade nodded. "It was before Emily and I decided to marry. Now we'll use the mortgage money to finance the repairs that have been needed for some time."

Lucas was beginning to understand where the conversation was headed. "I didn't come here to claim anything, Emily. I only came to see you. To make sure you're okay."

Her smile was radiant. "I'm so glad you did. Still, there are several things here that belonged to your mother, Lucas, and a few of Dad's personal belongings. If any of them have any sentimental value for you, you're welcome to whatever you want."

Her generosity touched him. She didn't owe him anything. She had every reason to be angry with him. But if she was, she hid it well.

"I don't want anything," he said quietly. "Knowing you're well and happy is all I'd hoped to gain."

"I'm happy," she assured him again.

He quickly changed the subject, finding talk of inheritances uncomfortable. "So, when are you two getting married?"

"We had hoped to be married before Christmas, but Wade's been so busy as police chief that we had to put it off until New Year's Eve. Now I think we were meant to wait for you. Please say you can stay for my wedding, Lucas."

Lucas frowned at the news that Wade Davenport was Honoria's chief of police. He'd assumed the guy was just a cop. "I wasn't really planning to stay that long."

He saw disappointment darken her eyes, but she managed to hold on to her smile. "All right, I won't press. But if you decide to stay, Wade and I would love for you to be there."

Lucas thought she might well change her mind about that once she'd had a chance to think about it. Why would she want him at the wedding, where the guests would more likely be staring at *him* than at the bride? He hadn't forgotten the way the people of this town had looked at him. The way they'd condemned him with disdainful glances and vicious whispers.

He had not returned to Honoria to ruin his sister's wedding. He would hang around a day or two to make sure everything really was okay, and then he'd take off again.

"You'll at least stay for Christmas, won't you?" Emily's expression had turned pleading. "It would mean so much to me, Lucas. I've missed you."

"I wouldn't blame you if you hated me," he said, more gruffly than he'd intended. "I left you to deal with all the baggage I left behind."

She met his gaze steadily. "I've been angry with you at times—maybe I still am, a little—but I've never hated you, Lucas. Even at eleven, I understood why you had to go. I didn't really blame you then, and I don't now. But I don't want to lose you again so soon, now that you've come back. Please say you'll stay for Christmas. It's only a few days away."

Hell. If it meant that much to her, he guessed he would have to stay. He supposed he owed her that much, at least.

"I'll stay for Christmas," he said. "If you're sure you want me to."

She beamed at the victory. "Oh, this is wonderful. I have my brother home for Christmas, and I'm only two weeks away from marrying the man I love. I've never been happier."

The two men responsible for her elation gave each other long, measuring looks.

After a moment, Wade glanced at his watch. "It's getting late. Clay and I have to get going. Er…where were you planning to stay, Lucas?"

"I'll probably get a room in one of those new motels west of town."

"You'll do no such thing." Emily spoke with a new determination. "You'll stay here, in the house where you grew up. This is still your home, too, Lucas."

Wade cleared his throat. "Um, technically…."

She rounded on him. "Don't even try to make me rescind my invitation. He's my brother, Wade. Would you make your sister stay in a tacky motel?"

"You haven't seen your brother since you were a child," Wade retorted. "I'm just saying I think it would be better if…"

"You might have noticed that on this particular point, I didn't *ask* what you think."

Lucas grimaced. Great. Now he'd caused a quarrel between his sister and her fiancé. He really should have just ignored that inexplicable impulse to return to Honoria. "I'll stay in the motel. I really don't mind."

Emily glared at him. "*I* mind. What kind of Southern hospitality is it when family has to stay in a motel? And at Christmas, too!"

She was just getting warmed up. "Grandmother McBride would be spinning in her grave. Aunt Bobbie and Uncle Caleb would probably come after you and insist that you stay with them if your own sister turned you out on the streets. As big as this house is, with all these empty bedrooms just waiting to be used, why in the world would I send my brother to a cold, impersonal motel room?"

Both Lucas and Wade were smiling ruefully by the time Emily ran out of breath. Clay was watching in wide-eyed fascination.

Lucas looked at Wade and spoke before she started again. "I think I've gotta stay here."

Wade nodded gravely. "I think you're right."

He set his empty glass on the tray and turned to his son. "Ready to go, Clay?"

"I sure will be glad when we live here," Clay muttered, climbing reluctantly off the couch.

Lucas saw the heat in Wade's eyes when he looked at Emily. "So will I, son," he murmured. "So will I."

Emily blushed happily. "I'll walk you guys out to the Jeep."

Clay took her hand. "'Bye, Uncle Lucas," he called over his shoulder as the family-to-be headed for the door.

"Yeah, er, see you, Clay."

Cute kid, he thought. He wondered how long it would be before Emily and Wade gave him a brother or sister. And didn't *that* thought make him feel old? Lucas still tended to think of Emily as his baby sister.

He spent the fifteen minutes while Emily was outside looking around, first studying the collection of antique Santa figurines on the mantel, a few of which looked familiar, and then the old photographs displayed on the sideboard. One photo, in particular, held his attention. It was a candid snapshot of himself at about thirteen, holding his little sister's hand. Dressed in lace, bows, and ruffles, four-year-old Emily held an enormous Easter basket and strained against Lucas's hand, eager to begin the search for colored eggs and candy.

He remembered that day. The family had gathered at Grandmother McBride's for Easter. Excited children had been underfoot, the table had almost groaned beneath the weight of all the food, the adults had been relaxed and happy. Even Josiah McBride Jr., Lucas's dour, emotionally withdrawn father, had been in a fairly good mood that day. And tiny, motherless Emily, so sweet and pretty in the dress Lucas had wrestled her into before church, had basked in the loving attention she received from her grandmother, aunts, uncles and cousins.

A hand fell on Lucas's arm, drawing him abruptly back to the present. Her hair a bit tousled, Emily looked from the photograph he'd been studying to his face. "I'm so glad you're here, Lucas. We have so much catching up to do."

He turned away from the photos. "Why don't

we save it for tomorrow? It's late, and I know you must be tired."

She nodded. "I'll take tomorrow afternoon off work. We can spend that time getting to know each other again."

"Sounds good. I'll go out to my car and grab my bag."

"I'll put out fresh sheets. I'm still using my old bedroom for now. Er…would you like the master bedroom? It's the only one with a king-size bed."

"I'll take my old room, if it's available." Lucas had no desire to sleep in his father's former bedroom. The cold-hearted bastard's ghost would probably haunt him.

Outside, he stood for a few long moments with his hand on the trunk of his car, listening to the familiar sounds of the rural Georgia night. Crickets, frogs, the occasional hoot of an owl or distant baying of a dog. The old house was surrounded by acres of uncleared woods, which he knew were alive with deer, raccoons, opossums, squirrels, and other wild creatures.

The happiest times of his youth had been spent in those woods, tracking animals, fishing in the creek, or sitting in his favorite "thinking place" in the branches of the big oak.

Memories. They crowded his mind no matter how hard he tried to push them away. A few good ones—but even more bad ones.

He shouldn't have come back. What the hell had he thought he would do? What had made him think Emily needed him, when it was obvious that she'd been getting along just fine on her own?

What he wanted to do was climb behind his

steering wheel and get the hell away from Honoria and the memories it held for him. He might have done just that, had he not suddenly realized that Emily was standing in the open front door, watching him as though she was afraid he might decide to leave without a goodbye again.

He couldn't do it to her. He'd hurt her enough the first time; he wouldn't ruin her Christmas or cast a pall over her wedding just because he was an emotional coward. He waved a hand to her and opened the trunk, hauling out his bag.

At least, he thought, he wouldn't have to see Rachel Jennings while he was in town.

That was one old memory he simply wasn't prepared to face.

2

RACHEL JENNINGS couldn't have explained why she'd been compelled to drive to the overlook Monday morning. Technically, the scenic point was on McBride land—it had once belonged to Lucas's grandparents, and now to his uncle, Caleb—but it could be reached by way of a country lane that turned off the main highway into town. The woods surrounding the area blended into the twenty acres once owned by Lucas's late father—and now, Rachel assumed, by Emily. A well-worn footpath led from the overlook to the house in which Lucas and Emily had been raised.

Once a prime spot for hiking, picnicking and teenage necking, the overlook had been made off-limits to trespassers fifteen years ago—right after Rachel's brother died there.

Without pausing, Rachel drove past the Do Not Enter signs. A few yards down the road, the woods seemed to close in behind her, cutting off her view of the highway. As a teenager, she'd loved driving her battered old Mustang past that point of visual contact with the world outside these woods. She'd been romantic and fanciful then, and she'd imagined that the trees had welcomed her, conspiratorially hiding her from disapproving eyes. And at the end of the lane, she'd known *he* would be waiting for her.

He wouldn't be waiting this time. Lucas McBride had vanished into the night fifteen years ago and no one in town—not even his family—had heard from him since. At least, that's what Rachel had been told by some of the avid gossips in town. Rachel hadn't asked about Lucas on this visit—not that she would have, anyway. But the gossips had been all too eager to bring up old scandals and probe for a reaction from Rachel.

Which was exactly why Rachel had avoided coming back to Honoria for so many years. She'd dealt with too much scandal in her teen years. She had allowed gossip to dictate her actions then, but she'd long since stopped basing her behavior on what anyone else might say about her.

She'd also grown accustomed to spending her Christmases alone in her apartment in Atlanta, except for brief, stilted visits with her mother in Carrollton every Christmas Eve. She would have been perfectly content to spend this holiday the same way, had not family obligations interfered. Her maternal grandmother had grown too frail to live alone, and planned to move into a retirement home close to Rachel's mother after the first of the year. Feeling a bit guilty because she'd stayed away from Honoria—and her grandmother—for so long, Rachel had volunteered to help settle the details.

She braked when she came to a gate blocking the road, yards short of the bluff she'd impulsively decided to visit. The gate hadn't been there fifteen years ago. The McBrides had apparently gotten serious about keeping people off this land.

Turning off the engine, she sat with her hands on the steering wheel for several long moments, staring at the gate and the road beyond. The same impulse that had brought her here made her open the door and climb out of the car, zipping up her lined denim jacket against the cold morning air.

She'd met Lucas here on winter mornings like this during her senior year of high school. Bundled in coats, scarves, hats and gloves, they'd snuggled together for warmth, their breath mingling in the air as they'd gazed off the bluff and planned a future together.

Lucas had been two years older than Rachel, and she had adored him. He'd been handsome and exciting, tough and complex. His notorious temper hadn't concerned her, since he'd never turned it against her. With her, he'd been gentle, caring—sweet, even—a side of him she knew few people saw.

She'd actually admired his rebellious spirit, envying him his freedom and courage. No one had made Lucas McBride do anything he didn't want to do. Rachel had been just the opposite. Back then, she'd been the dutiful daughter, the teacher's pet, the honor student and role model. Sneaking around to see Lucas had been the only act of rebellion she'd ever committed.

Feeling a touch of that old recklessness now, she approached the gate, noting that it would be easy enough to climb over. She put a hand on the top rail. She knew the gate was there for a reason, just as those Do Not Enter signs had been—but she wasn't in the mood to meekly follow rules at the moment.

She was still telling herself what a bad idea this was when she rested a booted foot on the bottom rail and stepped up. It was as if she were compelled to finish this pilgrimage into the past.

Maybe if she faced the memories again, they would stop haunting her. Surely fifteen years was long enough to pay for the foolish mistakes of her youth.

She dropped lightly onto the ground on the other side of the gate, pleased and rather surprised by how easily she'd scaled it. Not bad for a thirty-three-year-old accountant.

She didn't race up the path as she had at eighteen, but took her time walking the rest of the way to the overlook. It really was a beautiful morning. Birds sang from the tree branches overhead, and something rustled in the underbrush to her left— deer?—squirrel? She paid little attention to the noises, her attention focused on her objective.

The lane ended at the edge of the rock bluffs that loomed thirty feet above a wide, rushing creek. On the other side, the land rose again, climbing into more wooded acreage that had once belonged to McBrides, but had since passed into other hands.

Lucas had talked of buying that land, she remembered now. He'd wanted to build a house at the very top of the rise, with a deck overlooking the bluffs and the creek. He'd be able to feed the deer and squirrels from his porch, he'd said. Drink his morning coffee in the serenity of a crisp Georgia morning.

She wondered if Lucas had ever found the peace he'd craved.

A narrow footpath, worn by generations of hikers, ran along the edge of the bluffs. Rachel's steps slowed as she followed that path, her boots crunching on rocks and twigs. She wondered if the old stone structure she and Lucas had spent hours in would still be standing after so long. Had the McBrides torn it down to further discourage trespassers?

But when she pushed past a straggly evergreen half blocking the little-used path, she saw that the old building was still intact, if considerably more weathered than the last time she'd seen it.

Built in the fifties by Lucas's grandfather, Josiah McBride Sr., the ten-by-twelve structure resembled a gazebo or small pavilion built entirely of native stone. She and Lucas had always called it "the rock house." Small openings in the walls allowed fresh air to circulate through. Moss had formed on the floor and walls, making the shelter look as though it had sprouted from the forest floor. Rock benches lined the inside walls, providing shaded rest for weary hikers, a quiet place to commune with nature and escape the stress of everyday life.

It had made a very romantic meeting place for two young lovers kept apart by family hostility.

Rachel realized she was holding her breath as she slipped through the open doorway. Her heart was suddenly, inexplicably racing, the way it had on those earlier, happier visits to this place. She exhaled deeply when she stepped into the shelter to find it predictably empty, except for piles of dead leaves, as well as evidence of four-legged visitors.

Lucas had always kept the shelter swept out. He'd made sure the benches were clean so that Rachel's clothes wouldn't be soiled when she sat on them with him. The last time they'd been together here had been a stormy Saturday, a week after Rachel graduated from high school. The rain had fallen steadily outside, showering musically from the leaves of the trees surrounding them, but they'd been cozy and dry inside the shelter.

Lucas had brought a picnic lunch, and they'd spent several stolen hours talking, laughing, kissing—and reading aloud from a book of poetry Rachel had brought with her.

A wan smile curved her mouth as she remembered Lucas's initial skepticism about the poetry. He'd listened at first to humor her—he'd have done anything to please her then—and had read to her when she'd asked with halting self-consciousness. But by the end of that day, Rachel had thought Lucas was developing a budding appreciation for the verses she loved.

That day had been so innocent and romantic, so incredibly perfect that Rachel still got a lump in her throat when she remembered it. At the end of the afternoon, Lucas had told her that he wanted to marry her—as soon as she obtained her degree from Georgia Tech and he earned enough money to support them.

Crossing her arms tightly over her chest, Rachel leaned against a cold stone wall and gazed through one of the window openings. She was only marginally aware of anything she saw outside the structure; her mind was focused on the memories she'd hoped to exorcise by coming here.

Twenty feet from where she stood, an outcropping of mossy rock jutted over the sheer drop to the creek below. Rachel drew her jacket more snugly around her, feeling the cold penetrate to her bones.

Her older brother, Roger, had died in a fall from that very spot, soon after that blissful afternoon.

Rachel hadn't been very close to Roger, who'd been a moody, argumentative, difficult young man of twenty-one, but his death had shattered the world as she'd known it at eighteen. She had lost her only sibling. Her mother, Jane, already embittered by the desertion of her husband years earlier, had drawn so far into herself that no one had truly been able to reach her since. And Lucas, the man Rachel had secretly loved, was the prime suspect in Roger's death.

Rachel had never been alone with Lucas again. Less than eight weeks after Roger's death, Lucas was gone, leaving without a word of explanation. Rachel had escaped to college that fall, and before the year was over, her mother, too, had moved away from Honoria and its tragic history.

Rachel suddenly realized that if she'd hoped to put the past behind her by visiting this place today, she'd wasted her time. The memories were as painfully vivid as ever. It wasn't hard to imagine Lucas standing in the doorway, watching her with that brooding, hungry look that had always made her tremble in response.

With a faint sigh, she straightened, ran a hand through her long, dark hair, and turned toward the doorway.

Her heart nearly stopped when she saw the man standing there, watching her with narrowed, expressionless eyes.

This sharp-edged, hard-eyed, dangerous-looking man was not the passionate young rebel she'd fallen in love with in this shelter, she thought as she lifted a hand to her pounding heart.

But she had no doubt that he was Lucas Mc-Bride.

LUCAS THOUGHT he was hallucinating.

Or dreaming.

Rachel stood before one of the window openings, bathed in the pale, cool light of the December morning, huddled into a denim jacket that didn't conceal her willowy slenderness. Her dark, past-shoulder-length hair gleamed in the watery sunlight. He remembered how he'd once loved to bury his face and hands in it.

She looked exactly the way he remembered her.

It was like stepping into the past, and being dealt a blow to the heart.

And then she turned and looked at him, and he saw that this was no dewy-eyed, shyly eager, naively trusting, eighteen-year-old girl. This was a woman who'd known grief, hurt, betrayal, disappointment. The innocence and eagerness were gone from her dark-chocolate eyes—as, God knew, they were long gone from his own, if they'd ever existed there.

She was still beautiful.

Her eyes widened in surprise and a touch of what might have been fear when she saw him. He watched as instant recognition crossed her face. Maybe he hadn't changed outwardly as much as he'd thought, since Emily and Rachel had both known him so quickly.

Inwardly—well, his youth had been left in the past, along with his dreams and optimism.

It appeared Lucas was going to have to be the one to speak since Rachel seemed stunned into silence by his appearance. He thought it was a minor miracle that his voice came out fairly normal.

"Hello, Rachel."

Her mouth moved. No sound emerged.

He took a step forward. "You are the last person I expected to find here today."

If he'd known she would be here, would he still have come? He didn't like the cowardly way his silent answer made him feel.

"Lucas?" Her voice was a mere thread of sound.

He nodded, unable to force a smile. "It's been a long time."

Stupid thing to say, he thought irritably. But nothing else had come to him.

"Yes." She lifted a hand to her throat, as if to force strength into her voice. Fine tremors shook her fingers.

Hell, was she *afraid* of him?

He shoved his hands into the pockets of the black leather jacket he wore. "I didn't know you were in town. I heard you'd moved away."

He could almost see the willpower it took for her to regain her composure, to lift her chin and speak clearly and coolly. "It's my first visit back in a long time. I have family business to attend to. I'm certainly surprised to see *you* here."

He'd left in the middle of the night. Without telling her goodbye. He saw the accusations reflected in her eyes, and he reacted with guilty defensiveness. What had she expected from him? The one time he'd tried to communicate with her after her brother's death, she'd refused to talk to him.

Had she wanted him to grovel? Had she expected him to beg her to believe him innocent of everything being said about him in town?

He had thought she'd known him better than that.

"I came back to see my sister."

Rachel leaned slightly against the stone wall behind her. "I've heard Emily is getting married soon."

"New Year's Eve. She's marrying the new police chief." Lucas couldn't quite say that with a straight face; he felt his mouth twist wryly.

Rachel's smile was fleeting. "Did you come back to congratulate her or try to talk her out of marrying a cop?"

"I came back to make sure she's okay." It was the truth—just not all the truth.

"And is she?"

"She's fine. She seems happy."

"Was she glad to see you?"

Lucas relived that moment when Emily had thrown herself into his arms, startling him with the genuine warmth of her welcome. "I believe she was."

"And how is everyone else reacting to your reappearance?"

He shrugged. "I haven't seen anyone else. Except you. And I wouldn't describe your reaction as overjoyed."

Rachel looked out the window again. "I don't know how I'm feeling right now," she admitted quietly.

He understand that, since he couldn't have described his own emotions at the moment.

Something made him take another step toward her. "Rachel…"

Losing the thin veneer of bravado she'd assumed before, she flinched.

Lucas froze.

"Are you afraid of me?" he asked after a moment, his tone sounding flat, even to his own ears.

There was a long, taut pause, and then Rachel answered, her eyes downcast. "Yes."

Funny. Lucas thought he'd become so cynical during the past fifteen years that no one could ever hurt him again.

He'd been wrong.

He moved backward toward the doorway. His voice was gruff when he spoke.

"In my whole life, there have been only two people I would have died for. My sister is one. You're the other."

He didn't wait around for her response, but turned abruptly on one booted heel and headed back down the path toward his sister's house.

LUCAS HAD BEEN back at the house less than half an hour when he heard Emily's car in the driveway. She'd promised to be home for lunch. It was straight-up noon when she walked into the house, her arms loaded.

"I brought food," she said with a smile. "Chicken, mashed potatoes with gravy, fried okra, corn on the cob, biscuits, and peach cobbler for dessert. I remember that used to be your favorite meal. I hope you still like it."

It *was* one of his favorite meals, though one he rarely indulged in. "How could you possibly remember these things?" he demanded. "You were just a little girl when I left."

Her smile was both sweet and sad. "I remember everything about you, Lucas. Didn't you know how much I adored you?"

He didn't know what to say. He reached out, instead, to relieve her of the packages. "Where do you want these? Dining room or kitchen?"

"Kitchen. We can be more comfortable in there. I'll be in as soon as I put my purse away and wash my hands."

Lucas had the table set and the food ready to serve by the time Emily joined him.

"That was quick," she said with a smile, reaching for the refrigerator door. "What would you like to drink?"

"Do you have any tea made up?"

She pulled out a heavy glass pitcher half-filled with amber liquid. "I always have tea. I'm hooked on it, year-round."

"That sounds good." Watching her pour tea over two glasses of ice, Lucas could smell the chicken and cobbler waiting on the table. His mouth almost watered in anticipation. "It's great to have a real Southern meal again."

"It would be even better in the summertime, if these veggies were fresh-picked and we had a tomato right off the vine to slice on the side, but I figured this would do in a pinch. It came from Cora's Café—still one of the best eating places in town."

"It looks great." He began to fill his plate.

"You said it's good to have a Southern meal

again. Where have you been living all this time, Lucas?"

"California, mostly. Fried okra's a bit hard to come by there."

"California." She looked a bit dazzled as she dipped her fork into her potatoes. "Do you like it there?"

He shrugged. "It's okay."

"What do you do? For a living, I mean."

He kept his eyes on his plate. "I'm in computers."

"Computers? You're a programmer?"

"I've developed some software."

"Really? That sounds interesting. As I recall, you were fascinated with early video game technology. Your old Atari game is still around here somewhere—in the attic, I think. Do you remember teaching me to play Pac-Man and Space Invaders?"

"I remember." She'd sat in his lap in front of the old cabinet TV, her little hand clutching the joystick, her young brow furrowed in concentration.

"Did you miss me, Lucas?" A little girl's wistfulness echoed in her voice.

"Very much." The simple answer felt so inadequate to describe how much Lucas had missed his little sister, but it seemed to satisfy her.

"I'm glad." She nudged the box of chicken closer to him. "Have another piece. I bought plenty."

He didn't need to be urged twice.

Not visibly discouraged by Lucas's reticence, Emily returned to her questioning, eager to learn more about him. "You never married?"

"No."

"Do you have a girlfriend?"

"No."

"Are you gay?"

Appalled, Lucas choked and looked quickly up at her. "God, no."

She giggled. "Well, *that* got a reaction out of you, anyway."

She looked so much like the mischievous little girl he remembered that Lucas's chest tightened. "Brat."

Her blue eyes warmed, softened. Her smile turned misty. "That's what you always used to call me when I teased you."

"It still fits."

"I'm so glad you're home, Lucas."

He couldn't deal with any more emotion at the moment. He decided to turn the questioning back to her. "Did you tell anyone I'm here?"

"Did you want me to keep it a secret?"

He gave her return question a moment's consideration before answering. "I don't know."

"I didn't tell anyone. I simply said I had some business to attend to. Everyone at the bank assumed it was something to do with my wedding, and the people at the café thought I was buying lunch for myself and Wade."

He studied her closely. "Why didn't you tell anyone I'm here?"

Had it been for his sake, or her own?

"I suppose I just wanted to keep you to myself for a little while. I thought we'd call Aunt Bobbie and Uncle Caleb later. I know they'll want to see you."

Somewhat doubtfully, Lucas pictured his plainspoken country-lawyer uncle and bossy, school-teacher aunt. "You think so?"

"Of course they will. Lucas, they're your family."

Fifteen years on his own had almost made him forget what it was like to be part of a family. "Maybe Caleb and Bobbie will want to see me, but I can't think of anyone else who'll turn out to welcome me. I wasn't exactly the most popular guy in this town."

"Martha Godwin would be here in a flash if she heard you'd come back," Emily murmured, wrinkling her nose.

"Hell, is that nosy old biddy still around? She was the worst gossip in town when I was a kid."

"She still is," Emily admitted. "But she's not all bad, Lucas. She's just…nosy."

"How have you been treated by the locals, Emily? Did anyone hold it against you that you're a McBride? My sister?"

"And Nadine's daughter," she reminded him. "I've heard my share of comments about you both—but you expected that, I'm sure."

He nodded. "Yeah. But I'd hoped with both of us gone, the gossip would eventually fade away."

She frowned. "Is that why you left? To protect me from the gossip?"

Rachel's face hovered in Lucas's mind. "One of the reasons."

Emily shredded a biscuit onto her plate. "I would much rather have had you here."

He swallowed. "Were you treated well?" he persisted.

"On the whole, everyone's been kind. I've been

active in church, at work and in the community, and I have many friends. Honoria's grown since you left; there are a lot of people who know very little of the McBride history. With the exception of Sam Jennings and April Penny, for the most part, I've been treated with the same respect as anyone else."

"Sam Jennings?" Lucas almost spat the name. "Has that bastard given you a hard time?"

"Nothing I couldn't handle. He's a jerk, but I try not to let him get to me."

"Who's April Penny?"

"You might remember her as April Hankins, that's her maiden name. She's a few years older than I am—she'd have been about fourteen when you left town."

Lucas shook his head. "I don't remember her. I knew there was a family named Hankins who lived out on Culpepper Road."

"Same family. April's brother Vince was Savannah's high-school boyfriend. He was the football captain, class president, Mr. Popularity. And so conceited it's a wonder his football helmet fit over his big head."

Lucas swallowed a mouthful of still-warm peach cobbler and almost groaned in appreciation of the taste. "Sounds like he and our cousin Savannah were well-matched. Ernestine had her so spoiled, Savannah thought the world should be handed to her on a silver platter. And that she should be wearing a beauty-pageant tiara when she accepted it."

Emily smiled a little, but shook her head. "Savannah's changed a lot since you knew her, Lucas.

She had to grow up fast when she found herself pregnant with twins at seventeen. Raising them with no help from anyone but her mother put an end to her beauty-pageant days."

"Did the Hankins kid father the twins?"

"Yes, though he denied it. The entire Hankins family acted outraged at the suggestion that their son had behaved inappropriately. They implied that Savannah was a promiscuous tramp who wanted to trap Vince into marrying her. As if he was some great catch," she added scornfully.

"She had no doubt he fathered the kids?"

"Of course not. Savannah was devastated when Vince and his buddies told everyone she slept around. She swore Vince was the only one—and her family believed her."

"So how come she didn't get a blood test and prove it to everyone? Make the guy own up to his responsibilities?" Lucas had no respect for a man who would deny his own children. At least he could be confident that he hadn't left Rachel in that kind of trouble when he'd taken off fifteen years ago.

"Because she inherited as much of the McBride pride as she did their recklessness. She didn't want anything from Vince. And she didn't want to force any man to be a father to her children. She's been a good mother, Lucas. The twins are good kids. And now she's married to a man who appreciates all of them. He's Christopher Pace, the author. You might have heard of him."

Lucas lifted an eyebrow. He'd heard of Pace, even read a couple of the guy's books. "Sounds like everything turned out all right for her."

"Yes. Which made April even more hateful to me—to all the McBrides. She resents the idea that Savannah is now married to a wealthy, famous man while her precious brother is only a used-car salesman."

"Why should she take any of that out on you?"

"Who knows? She just doesn't like McBrides. It always seemed to irk her that I have more friends than she did, even though I was your sister and Nadine's daughter. She can't see it's because she's so spiteful that people tend to give her a wide berth."

Lucas had lost interest in April Hankins. It sounded to him as though Emily could hold her own against the woman. In fact, it sounded as if Emily had made a satisfying life for herself here despite her family's less-than-spotless reputation.

It had obviously been unnecessary for Lucas to come rushing back to Honoria. He could have stayed away. Could have avoided getting himself roped into a family Christmas—and seeing Rachel again. Hearing Rachel admit that she was afraid of him.

"What do people say about me in town?"

Emily busied herself clearing away the remains of their lunch. "Oh, you know…they wonder whatever became of you. Why you left so abruptly."

He covered her hand with his, stilling her movements. "Emily. What do they say about me and Roger Jennings?"

She cleared her throat. "Some of them—especially Sam Jennings and his friends—say you got away with…with…"

"With murder." Lucas could say it, even if his sister could not.

"Yes."

He kept his hand on hers. "I didn't kill Roger."

Her gaze met his, and he was relieved to see that there was no shadow of doubt in her eyes. "I never for a moment believed you did. And neither does anyone else with half a brain. If there had been any evidence to link you to Roger's death, Chief Packer would have found it. He certainly tried hard enough to find a reason to arrest you. But there was no evidence, and you had an alibi."

He released her hand. This time it was Lucas who looked away, uncomfortable by the mention of that "alibi."

"Whatever happened to Lizzie Carpenter?" he asked gruffly.

"She married a guy from Macon about ten years ago and moved away. She would never talk about you after you left. She tended to burst into tears whenever your name was mentioned, so people eventually stopped asking her about you."

Lucas winced. "Great. Everyone thought I slept with her, ruined her reputation, and then left town and broke her heart, right?"

"I've heard murmurs to that effect," Emily said almost apologetically.

Lucas shook his head, thinking of Rachel and re-membering the old pain he'd seen in her eyes. God, what a mess he'd made of things fifteen years ago.

The telephone rang. Emily reached for the kitchen extension. "Surely Martha Godwin hasn't already found out you're in town."

Lucas grimaced.

But it was immediately obvious from her besotted smile that the caller was her fiancé. "Lucas and I just finished lunch," she said. "We're having a very nice visit."

To give her privacy, Lucas motioned to his sister to take her time with her conversation and walked out the kitchen door.

He had a lot to think about, and he needed a few minutes alone to do so.

It had been a hell of a day. And it was only a little after noon.

3

THE BIG OAK TREE had to be well over a hundred years old. Its trunk was huge, gnarled, its branches spreading far out around it. Lightning had hit the tree at some point in its long history, leaving a thick scar down the north side. But the tree had endured.

Lucas didn't remember the first time he'd climbed that tree. He couldn't have been more than seven or eight. Some twenty feet up was a hollow formed by the juncture of several large, leafy branches. In the summertime, a boy could sit in that hollow, hidden from the world, and do a lot of thinking.

He remembered well the last time he'd sat in that spot. He'd been twenty. It had been an impulse of a young man who was desperately in love, frustrated, confused, angry, uncertain.

He'd had a quarrel with an angry Roger Jenkins that morning. Roger had found out that Lucas had been secretly meeting Rachel, despite a long history of animosity between the McBride and Jenkins families. Roger had been infuriated that his sister had been consorting with the stepson of the woman who'd seduced their father away from his family.

There'd been some pushing. Some shoving. Some threats.

Resting one hand against the trunk of the oak, Lucas closed his eyes, and he could almost hear Roger snarling, "Stay away from my sister, McBride. Or I'll kill you."

And Lucas had answered, with his usual reckless temper, "I'll kill *you* before I let you keep me from her."

"The same way your father killed his wife and my dad?"

Lucas's first reaction to Roger's question had been scorn. "What the hell are you talking about?"

Nine years earlier, Nadine McBride and Al Jennings had run off together. They hadn't been heard from since. Roger had been convinced that his father, Al, would never have voluntarily abandoned his children. "If he was alive, he would have called. He would have wanted to see us. I think your father caught my dad with your slut of a stepmother and killed them both."

"And I think you're out of your mind."

Roger had sworn then that he would find proof. "And when I do, your father will go to prison. And my sister will never let you near her again."

They'd parted after a few more angry snarls and empty threats. Needing to cool off before facing his family, Lucas had come impulsively to the old oak tree where he'd spent so many quiet hours as a boy. The hollow had still held him, hidden him from view. Given him a private place to get his temper under control and contemplate Roger's ridiculous accusations.

He'd been sitting there perhaps half an hour

when his little sister and their cousins, Savannah
and Tara, had trudged into the clearing, toting an
old cypress trunk between them. From his vantage
point, Lucas could see and hear them as they'd giggled and chattered and dug in the rain-softened
ground with shovels borrowed from his father's
tool shed.

Shamelessly eavesdropping on the conversation,
Lucas had discovered that the girls had designated
the trunk as a "time capsule," to be dug up in fifteen years on Savannah's birthday—a time so far in
the future they could hardly imagine it. Before burying the trunk, they'd opened it to make sure the
contents were securely wrapped. Lucas had
learned that each girl had packed an individual
box of "treasures," written their names on the tops
with permanent markers, and wrapped the boxes
in plastic garbage bags to protect them inside the
trunk.

He'd found the little ceremony amusing, a welcome distraction from his personal problems. He'd
thought Emily was so cute tagging along with her
older cousins, imitating their speech and behavior,
participating so eagerly in burying the trunk. He
had wondered if they would remember to dig up
the trunk in fifteen years, or if it would be long forgotten by then.

Now, after reading the article in the Honoria *Gazette* and learning that a heavy gold bracelet had
been stolen from Emily in a recent home break-in,
Lucas knew that the trunk had, indeed, been un-
earthed.

Lucas himself had hidden that bracelet in Emily's time capsule only two weeks after the girls

had buried it. It had been the day after Roger Jennings fell from the bluff—less than two months before Lucas left town vowing never to return.

What had Emily thought when she found it? Who had taken it from her, and where was it now?

Those were the questions that had brought Lucas back to Honoria, questions he hadn't found quite the right time to ask.

"Lucas?"

It took Lucas a moment to make the transition from past to present. Emily-the-child faded into memory as Emily-the-woman approached her brother. Bundled into a down-filled parka, she carried his leather jacket in her arms. "Aren't you getting cold out here without your jacket?"

He *was* cold, actually. He was just so caught up in his thoughts, he hadn't realized it. He took the jacket and shrugged into it, touched by her concern. It had been a long time since anyone had worried about him.

Emily tucked her hands into her pockets and looked around. "Checking out the old grounds?"

"Yeah. Hasn't changed much."

"No. Not much." Her gaze drifted to the bare patch of earth where the chest had once been buried.

Lucas didn't mention the time capsule, since Emily didn't know he'd seen her bury it. Instead, he asked another question.

"What did the old man tell you about me, Emily?"

She looked surprised. "Dad?"

He nodded.

"Nothing. He never mentioned you at all. I

sometimes wondered if you and he had a fight before you left. Did you?"

Lucas wouldn't have called it a fight. A confrontation, maybe. It had ended with Josiah telling his son he never wanted to see him again. Lucas hadn't gotten any of his questions answered, but he had learned once and for all that Josiah was incapable of loving anyone—something both of Josiah's wives must have discovered on their own.

"Dad and I just didn't get along," was all he said to Emily.

"He couldn't seem to get along with anyone. I suppose the only reason he and I didn't quarrel is because I never challenged him. I learned to be quiet and good so everything would be peaceful."

Lucas grimaced. "Not much of a childhood for you. I'm sorry, Emily."

She shook her head. "It wasn't your fault. You did what you had to do. Even though I never stopped missing you, I had people here to love me. Aunt Bobbie and Uncle Caleb were always nearby when I needed them, and that meant a great deal to me."

"I want to thank them for that before I leave again."

Emily sighed. "I don't like to think about you leaving. But I'd like to call Aunt Bobbie and Uncle Caleb to tell them you're here. Their feelings will be hurt if they hear it first from someone else."

"You can tell them tomorrow," Lucas conceded somewhat reluctantly. Though he rather dreaded the extended family reunion, he knew Emily had her heart set on the family being together for

Christmas. Lucas couldn't help feeling that he owed her this.

"I heard something today I think you should know," she said, seeming to broach the subject carefully. "Rachel Jennings is in town for the holiday."

It took a massive effort for Lucas not to react visibly to the name. As far as he knew, no one except Roger had learned that Lucas and Rachel had been involved. How could Emily possibly have found out?

"Er…why did you think I should know that?" he asked, his tone carefully neutral.

"She *is* Sam Jennings's niece. I'm sure Sam has tried to poison Rachel's mind against us, the same way he has tried to influence others. If she blames you for what happened to her brother, it could get awkward if you run into her unexpectedly. I just want you to be prepared."

Lucas wished he'd been prepared before he *had* run into Rachel. He couldn't forget the way she'd flinched when he'd stepped toward her.

He hadn't been prepared for her fear. Did she really think he would ever do anything to hurt her?

"She wouldn't be the only one in town who blames me for Roger's death." Lucas was unable to keep the bitterness out of his voice. "Believe me, Emily. I know what to expect."

Emily sighed and placed a hand on his arm. "I'm sorry you were treated so badly here, Lucas. It wasn't fair for people who didn't even know you to judge you so harshly."

Lucas had once thought Rachel knew him better

than anyone in the world. And still she'd judged him—and had obviously found him guilty.

He cleared his throat. "We'd better get back to the house. I imagine your cop boyfriend will be showing up before long."

Emily giggled. "My cop fiancé," she corrected him. "I hope you and Wade can become friends, Lucas."

"Me, friends with a cop. It would be a first—but for you, I'll try."

"Thank you."

Lucas looked around the clearing one more time, deliberately avoiding looking toward the path that led toward the stone shelter and the bluffs. He would go back there, of course, but tonight he needed to put his talk with Rachel out of his mind.

He exhaled deeply and turned to his sister. "Your nose is getting pink. Let's go inside."

Emily tucked her hand beneath his arm and matched her steps to his, walking close to his side.

His sister made it very clear that she wasn't afraid of him, he mused.

Why the hell was Rachel?

FROM THE BIG WOODEN rocker on her grandmother's front porch, Rachel could see the festive lights strung on the neighbors' houses. Most had decorated lavishly for Christmas this year. The house next door had a Santa in a sleigh with all eight reindeer on the roof, surrounded by blinking lights and glittering illuminated "icicles." Farther down the street, she spotted plastic snowmen, a couple of Nativity scenes, some animated carolers, and trees decorated with lights and ornaments.

Finding the festive display oddly depressing, Rachel looked away from the scene.

There were no colored lights on her grandmother's house. Jenny Holder would be moving in less than a month, and hadn't wanted to bother with Christmas decorations this year. Easily tired these days, she'd turned in early, leaving Rachel alone and wide-awake at just after 9:00 p.m. When the house had become too close and quiet, Rachel had pulled on her coat and come outside, hoping the night air would soothe her.

She knew she would never sleep as long as Lucas's words kept echoing in her mind.

In my whole life, there have been only two people I would have died for. My sister is one. You're the other.

Just as she couldn't forget his words, she was haunted by the look on his face when he had asked her if she was afraid of him. When she had answered that she was.

She'd hurt him. As hard and intimidating as he'd appeared, she had hurt him with her candid, one-word answer. And now, idiot that she was, she was feeling guilty about it.

She didn't owe Lucas McBride apologies or explanations, she reminded herself. Exactly the reverse was true. She'd had every reason to verbally flail him for the way he'd hurt her fifteen years ago—to tell him exactly what she thought of him for causing her so much pain. To say all the things she'd fantasized about saying on those nights when she'd lain awake, remembering and seething with anger.

How many times had she played that scene in her head during her college years, before she'd finally decided it was time to put the past behind her and build a life for herself?

But no matter how hard she tried, she couldn't forget the way he'd looked when he'd walked out of that stone shelter.

RACHEL HAD NO WAY of knowing, of course, that Lucas would go to the rock house Tuesday morning. Even as she climbed over the gate and trudged down the path, she found herself hoping he wouldn't be there.

At least she could have told herself that she'd made an effort to apologize.

But whatever impulse had forced her there that morning must have affected Lucas, as well. He stepped into the doorway just as Rachel reached it.

She couldn't help studying his face, searching for the Lucas she'd known so long ago. Back then, he'd worn his toast-brown hair long and shaggy, as untamed as his reputation. It was cut somewhat more conservatively now, though still just shaggy enough to give a hint of the rebel he'd been. She saw no evidence of gray in the brown, which was rather unfair, since she'd found a few strands lately in her own dark hair.

Time and frowns had carved lines around his eyes and mouth, which only made his lean, angular face even more fascinating than she'd remembered.

He didn't look particularly surprised by her appearance. Whether that was because he'd half expected her, or because he'd become so very good at masking his emotions, she didn't know.

Now that she was here, she hadn't the faintest idea what to say to him.

He had spoken first yesterday, when she'd been struck speechless by the sight of him. This time he was leaving it up to her. He crossed his arms over his chest and leaned against the doorway, looking prepared to stand there for hours if that's what it took.

Rachel laced her fingers tightly in front of her and cleared her throat. "There's something I need to say to you."

He moved just a little. Bracing himself? She couldn't tell from his expression.

"What is it?" His tone wasn't encouraging.

"What I said yesterday—about being afraid of you—I didn't mean it the way it sounded."

"And how do you think it sounded?"

He wasn't making this easy for her. She reminded herself that she didn't have to do this. The way he was acting, it would serve him right if she turned and walked away without another word.

But she sensed that she had hurt him yesterday and she couldn't help thinking part of his behavior was due to that. Lucas had always had a wild creature's instinct to draw more deeply into himself when he was wounded.

It bothered her more than a little that she still knew him so well, even after trying so hard and for so long to put him out of her mind.

Her annoyance with his behavior gave strength to her voice. She lifted her chin and looked him in the eye. "You knew I would come, didn't you? You were waiting for me."

"How could I have known that? When I left you yesterday, you were cowering in fear of me."

"I was *not* cowering! You startled me, that's all."

"Why did you really come here this morning, Rachel?"

She pushed her hands into the pockets of her lined denim jacket. "I told you. I came to apologize for what I said."

"You don't owe me an apology. What you said was the truth, wasn't it?"

It *had* been the truth, of course. Rachel wasn't afraid that Lucas would harm her physically—but on an emotional level, he terrified her. It had taken her years to get over Lucas McBride. To finally feel that she had put her girlhood dreams behind her and learned to be content with the life she'd built for herself.

She was no longer the naive young girl who had been so desperately in love with this man. But the fact that her pulse was racing now, her palms damp, her throat tight, warned her that she was still dangerously vulnerable where Lucas was concerned.

He had almost destroyed the girl. She didn't even want to think about what he could do to the woman.

She took a step backward. "I have to go."

"You're still afraid of me." Lucas's voice was as flat as his cold blue eyes.

She refused to answer, though pride made her lift her chin a little higher. "I have to go," she repeated.

"Fine. Run away from me, Rachel Jennings.

That's what you did before—and it mattered then."

The sudden bitterness in his voice almost made her gasp. He blamed *her* for what had happened between them fifteen years ago? Could he possibly be that arrogant?

"*You* were the one who left town without a word," she reminded him angrily. "You were the one who broke my heart. Don't even try to pretend I mattered to you. You fed me enough lies then, and I believed everything you said because I was in love with you. But I'm not as trusting now as I was then. And it's far too late for apologies."

His eyes narrowed. For the first time that morning, she saw emotion in them. And she almost recoiled from the sheer power of it.

"At least we agree on that," he almost snarled. "It's much too late for you to apologize."

This time she did gasp. For *her* to apologize?

He really was the most incredibly arrogant man she'd ever known. "Of all the—"

Lucas was in no mood, apparently, to prolong the quarrel. He simply walked past her and strode down the path toward the woods, disappearing into the trees without a backward glance.

Arrogance, she decided furiously, didn't begin to describe Lucas McBride.

LIES. Rachel had accused him of telling her lies fifteen years ago.

He'd poured his heart out to her, damn it. Bared his soul. Opened himself to her as he had to no one else, not even the little sister he'd cherished.

And Rachel accused him of telling her nothing but lies.

How could he have been so wrong about what they'd shared? Had he really been so naive that he'd believed her love for him was strong enough to survive a scandal?

It hadn't particularly surprised him when more than half the citizens of Honoria had believed him capable of murdering Roger Jennings. He'd become accustomed to their suspicions and dislike of him. Hell, he supposed he'd earned most of that with his quick temper and rebellious conduct.

But with Rachel he'd been different. He'd felt no need to put on a front for her. She'd never seemed to look down at him because his father was a thoroughly dislikable man, or because his stepmother had been the town whore. Rachel hadn't even blamed Lucas because his stepmother had hurt her family by running off with her father.

Roger had blamed the entire McBride family for Nadine's behavior.

But Rachel had been the first person to look beyond the bravado Lucas had assumed for the disapproving townspeople, and to find the real person inside him. Or so he had believed. If she really thought that he'd ever lied to her, or that he'd had anything to do with her brother's death, then she hadn't known him at all.

"You certainly look serious. What's wrong?"

Lucas hadn't even heard his sister enter the house. He looked up from the untouched cup of rapidly cooling coffee on the table in front of him to find Emily standing in the kitchen doorway, peeling off the coat she'd worn to work.

"Want a cup of coffee?" he asked, standing. "I just made a fresh pot."

"Sounds good. Thanks."

Lucas poured her a cup of the hot liquid and set it on the table across from his own. "How was your day?"

"Fine. But you haven't answered my question. Did something happen to upset you?"

He shrugged. "I've been dealing with some bad memories. Did you talk to Caleb and Bobbie?"

"I talked to Aunt Bobbie. She said she and Uncle Caleb will come by to see you this evening. She was so thrilled to hear you'd come back, and really surprised that no one in town even knows you're here yet."

"I imagine the word will get out soon enough. I hope there's no unpleasantness for you when it does."

Emily tossed her head. "Anyone who says anything ugly about you to me had better be prepared to deal with the consequences."

He regarded her with a faint, somewhat bemused smile. "I don't remember you being quite so ferocious fifteen years ago."

"I wasn't. I've only learned within the past year or so to stand up for myself and the people I care about. And you know what? It feels great."

He nodded. "Good for you."

"I even told Sam Jennings off a few weeks ago. He was so mad about failing to pin a theft charge on me that he said some really ugly things. He made some nasty cracks about you, and I finally had enough. I told him..."

"Wait a minute. You said Sam Jennings tried to pin a theft charge on you?"

She nodded. "One of his employees embezzled several thousand dollars from one of his business accounts, and he said I did it when the deposits were made at the bank where I work. He wanted Wade to arrest me on the spot, but Wade insisted on conducting an investigation first. I was completely cleared, of course, but it was as if Sam wanted me to be the guilty one. He really hates McBrides. When it comes to us, he isn't even rational."

"I can talk to him while I'm here. I guarantee you he'll never give you any more trouble after I'm finished with him."

"No. I told him off myself. And Wade threatened him with a slander suit if he kept spreading his vicious accusations around."

"How long have you known Wade?"

"I met him in September—just before Sam accused me of being a thief."

Lucas lifted his left eyebrow. "September of this year?"

"Yes. Three months ago."

"And when did you decide to get married?"

"Just before Thanksgiving."

"Rather fast, wasn't it?"

"Yes," she admitted. "But it just felt right, you know? I had the house for sale and I was ready to move out of Honoria. After Dad died, I was tired of taking care of other people. I wanted to do some traveling, see the world, be totally selfish."

"So you decided to marry a single father instead?"

She laughed softly. "Sounds like the exact opposite of what I'd planned, doesn't it?"

"Yeah. But you seem happy with your choice."

"I'm very happy. I was going away to find fulfillment, but then I realized that what I wanted was right here."

Lucas grimaced. "I'm glad *you* feel that way."

She reached across the table to cover his hand with hers. It still surprised him, at times, how affectionate she was with him.

"Honoria doesn't hold many happy memories for you, does it, Lucas? First your mother died and then your stepmother—my mother—humiliated the family by running off with another man. Dad was never particularly supportive of you. And then Roger Jennings died…. I don't blame you for wanting to get as far away from this town as possible."

She hadn't mentioned the worst thing that had happened to him here, because she had never known about his relationship with Rachel. And he had no intention of telling her about it now. "Not all the memories are bad ones. I have a lot of good memories of you."

She smiled at him. "That was a sweet thing to say."

"Yeah, well, I'm just a sweet guy."

She laughed. "Why, Lucas. I believe you just made a joke."

Her laugh hadn't changed in all this time, Lucas thought. It could still make him smile, could still bring some warmth to that cold place inside him.

The doorbell rang, causing Emily to jump to her

feet. "That's either Wade and Clay, or Aunt Bobbie and Uncle Caleb. I'll let them in."

Lucas rinsed out the coffee cups while Emily went to answer the door. He knew he was going to have to spend some time being sociable during the next few hours. But what he really wanted to do was go off by himself somewhere and give some more thought to the words Rachel had thrown at him that morning.

You were the one who broke my heart...I believed everything you said because I was in love with you.

When, exactly, had she stopped believing him? And why?

4

WADE WAS OBVIOUSLY surprised when Lucas walked into his office Wednesday morning, but he greeted him cordially enough.

"Hello, Lucas. How did you get past Mrs. Mosler? She never lets anyone in here without being announced."

Lucas shrugged. "I didn't need to be announced."

A flustered-looking, fifty-something woman appeared in the doorway behind Lucas, glaring at him before turning to her boss. "I'm sorry, Chief. I was taking a telephone call and this man just walked right past me without even pausing."

"That's all right, Mrs. Mosler. This is my future brother-in-law, Lucas McBride. He's probably here on family business."

Lucas watched as the woman paled. "Lucas McBride?" she repeated almost involuntarily.

Lucas nodded coolly. He was tempted to lean into her face, and say "Boo." She would probably faint if he did. As far as he remembered, he had never met this woman, but she had obviously heard of him.

"I'll, um, leave you two to visit," she said, hands fluttering. "Should I hold your calls, Chief?"

"I'll take the important ones." Wade waited until she had closed the door behind her, then waved Lucas toward a chair. "Have a seat. Want some coffee?"

"No, thanks." Lucas took one of the three chairs grouped around Wade's scarred and battered wooden desk—the same desk that had been there in Chief Packer's time, Lucas suspected. There'd been a few superficial changes made in the Honoria police department building, but most of it was all too familiar.

Lucas had once vowed never to enter the place again. He should have remembered the title to the old James Bond movie. *Never Say Never Again.*

Wade leaned back in his chair, his elbows on the arm rests, his fingers steepled in front of him. "Is there something you want to discuss with me, or are you just visiting all your old haunts today?"

"Very funny."

Wade chuckled. "I notice you didn't have any trouble finding your way to my office without directions."

"I probably know this place as well as you do. Seemed like every time I turned around, Packer was hauling me in for something."

"According to your file, you were only officially arrested a couple of times. You seemed to have a knack for getting into fights."

"They were never my fault."

"You'd be surprised how often I've heard that."

Lucas glanced at a somewhat shabby little artificial Christmas tree sitting on a table in one corner of Wade's office, someone's attempt at creating a festive atmosphere in the all-business environment. He would bet the nervous Mrs. Mosler had been responsible for the decorations.

"What can I do for you, Lucas?"

So much for small talk, apparently. Lucas had never been very good at it, anyway. "Tell me about what happened to Emily in October. I heard she was attacked."

Wade's eyebrows lifted. "She told you about that?"

"No. But I heard about it. I want you to tell me the details."

Lucas watched as Wade's eyes darkened and his expression clouded. "Emily walked into the house and was hit on the back of the head. She fell forward and hit a table. I found her unconscious a short while later."

"How badly was she hurt?"

"She had a mild concussion. She was treated and released from the hospital the same night, so her injuries were relatively minor." Wade rubbed a hand over his face. "My heart stopped when I found her lying on that floor. When I saw the blood, I..."

He stopped and cleared his throat.

Lucas found himself liking Wade Davenport a little more. Wade so obviously cared very deeply for Emily, and that, alone, was enough to earn him points in Lucas's estimation.

"I heard there was a rash of home break-ins around that time."

"Yeah. We had a few bored teenagers who decided it might be fun to start a burglary ring. The O'Brien kid, Kevin, was the ringleader. We caught them, and they confessed to most of the break-ins."

Catching an undertone in Wade's voice, Lucas frowned. "*Most* of the break-ins?"

"I could never get them to admit having anything to do with the one at Emily's house. They talked about every other break-in that had been reported, but swore they didn't go near Emily."

"Do you believe them?"

"There would be good reason for them to deny it, of course. Emily's was the only break-in that involved a physical attack. No one was home in any of the other incidents. It was just bad luck that Emily walked in on them."

"But..."

Wade sighed. "But it doesn't feel right. Never has. The break-in at Emily's place looked like a standard burglary scene—a TV and VCR were stacked on the floor ready to be carried out, her jewelry box had been dumped and searched, drawers were emptied. But in the other incidents, the kids broke in, grabbed everything in sight and took off. Whoever was in Emily's house took the time to conduct a pretty thorough search."

"As if he was looking for something in particular?"

Wade nodded, his gaze on Lucas's face. "It could have been seen that way."

"You said there were some things left piled on the floor. Was anything actually taken?"

"Some cash. A couple of pairs of gold earrings and a gold necklace. And the gold bracelet Emily was wearing when she walked in."

"Someone attacked her and then took the bracelet off her arm?"

"And left her lying unconscious on the floor."

Wade's jaw was rigid. "If I'd had proof of who did that to her, I'd have knocked his teeth in, even if it meant losing my badge."

Lucas wasn't sure he would let the guy off with only a few missing teeth. He had to rein in his anger to continue speaking in the objective tone he'd used so far. "I've noticed Emily's been wearing a gold bracelet every day since I arrived."

"I gave her that one after the robbery. The one stolen from her was an antique. Very heavy links, and an ornate oval clasp. It belonged to her mother."

Wade had just described the bracelet Lucas had buried in Emily's time capsule—confirming Lucas's suspicions that she had discovered it there.

"Now that I've told you everything I know about the break-in, why don't you tell *me* why you're so interested?"

Lucas shrugged. "My sister was attacked. Isn't it natural for me to be interested in making sure someone pays for it?"

"You have reason to believe Emily was specifically targeted?"

"That's what I'm asking *you*."

Wade's gaze narrowed on Lucas's face. "There's something you aren't telling me. How did you find out about the break-in, if Emily didn't tell you? You told your aunt and uncle last night that you haven't seen anyone else in town while you've been here."

Lucas shrugged.

"You knew your father had died. You didn't seem particularly surprised that Emily still lived in the same house. Have you been keeping tabs on her since you left?''

"I've reassured myself that she was all right. If she'd ever really needed me, I'd have been here."

"But you never came back, even for a visit. Not even for your father's funeral. What was it about the break-in that brought you back?"

Lucas stalled by turning the questioning back to Wade. "When did you decide I wasn't here to claim my share of my father's estate?"

"When I found out that you could buy up half of Honoria, if you wanted," Wade answered evenly.

Lucas scowled. "You've investigated me?"

"Yes. You've done all right for yourself, haven't you?"

His opinion of Wade Davenport slipped a notch. "Typical cop meddling."

"Typical fiancé meddling," Wade corrected him. "You aren't the only one needing reassurance that Emily's all right."

Lucas wasn't sure Emily would appreciate either of them being so overprotective of her, but he supposed he could forgive Wade, this time, for meddling, since he'd had Emily's welfare at heart. But how much could he trust the guy?

There was only one way to find out.

"I need a favor from you, Wade."

The immediate wariness that crossed Wade's face was not particularly flattering. "What kind of favor?"

"I want to see all the old files on Roger Jennings's death fifteen years ago. Everything Chief Packer found out."

For several long moments, there was no sound in

the office except the ticking of the old wooden clock on the wall behind Wade's head. Wade sat without moving, studying Lucas intently over his steepled fingers.

When he spoke, his voice was quiet, almost as if he was musing aloud. "What possible connection could Roger Jennings's death have to the break-in at Emily's house?"

At least his sister wasn't marrying a stupid man, Lucas thought. "Probably none. But I would still like to see the files."

"According to what I've read, Chief Packer was never fully convinced that you had nothing to do with Jennings's death. Had it not been for your alibi, you might well have found yourself facing charges."

Lucas nodded, knowing his scowl had deepened at the mention of his "alibi."

"The girl who claimed you spent the entire night with her had some inconsistencies in her story that bothered Packer. But he could never shake her. Even after you left town, apparently dumping her along with your family, she never recanted."

"I never asked her to defend me," Lucas muttered. In fact, Lizzie's well-intentioned "help" had caused almost as many problems as it had solved, but he wasn't about to go into that now.

"You're aware, of course, that there is no statute of limitations for murder."

"I did not kill Roger Jennings."

Lucas didn't know why he thought Wade would believe him when people who had known him a lot longer than the police chief had thought him guilty. Even Rachel apparently had her doubts, judging from her behavior.

Wade said only, "That's what your sister keeps telling me. She never doubted your innocence. I've pointed out, of course, that she was just a little girl when you left, and she might not have known you as well as she thought, but she almost took my head off. You were her hero fifteen years ago— and, like it or not, I'm not so sure that's changed much."

Lucas felt a quick rush of satisfaction, even though he knew he was no hero. But it was kind of nice to think there was one person in the world who could see him that way.

"Well, McBride? Are you going to tell me what you're hoping to find in those files?"

"Are you going to let me see them?" Lucas countered.

A whirring sound erupted from the clock on the wall, followed by the appearance of a whimsical wooden bird. Lucas winced when the thing let out several teeth-jarring "cuckoos."

"I'd have to kill that thing," he said without thinking.

"Some folks might think that was a revealing statement coming from you," Wade drawled. And then he pushed his chair away from his desk and stood. "I'm supposed to meet Emily for lunch at Cora's. I'm going to be late if I don't leave now. Why don't you join us?"

Lucas rose from his chair. "You haven't answered me about the files."

"I'll think about it. How about lunch?"

Lucas pushed his hands into the pockets of the

leather jacket he hadn't removed. "I doubt if Emily would enjoy her lunch with me there. Everyone in the place would be staring and whispering."

"If you think Emily would care about that, you haven't gotten to know her as well as I'd thought during the past couple of days. Are you going to hide from the gossips the whole time you're here?"

Lucas lifted his head sharply. "I don't hide from anyone."

Wade chuckled. "Damn. For a minute there, you looked just like Emily when she's in a temper. Come have lunch with us, Lucas. It'll make your sister happy. You and I will look through the old files later."

That sounded like a promise. Or maybe a bribe. For some reason, Wade seemed to want Lucas to make a public appearance. To find out how the townspeople reacted to him, maybe? Or how he reacted to *them*?

Whatever Wade's purpose, Lucas didn't see how he could decline. He motioned wryly toward the door. "After you."

Cora's Café was only a few blocks from the police station. Since it was a nice day, Wade and Lucas decided to walk. Lucas pulled his leather jacket tighter around his neck and stuck his hands in the pockets, making no effort to meet the eyes of anyone they passed. If any curious looks came their way, he didn't see them. He wasn't looking for familiar faces, and he would have been glad if no one recognized him.

The café was small, and two-thirds of the tables were occupied. Emily was waiting just inside the door. Her face lit up when she saw them.

"Lucas! What a nice surprise," she said, rushing to his side to kiss his cheek. And then she turned to offer a kiss to Wade. "I'm very glad to see you both."

Wade grinned and draped an arm around her shoulders. "Good thing you added that. I was beginning to feel slighted."

"With your ego? No way," his loving fiancée teased.

Lucas noticed that several of the diners had begun to look their way, smiling when they saw Emily and Wade, frowning in curiosity when they noticed Lucas. He could spot the people who recognized him—they were the ones whose jaws dropped or whose forks clattered suddenly on tabletops.

A broad-beamed, frizzy-permed waitress ambled toward them, carrying three plastic menus tucked under one arm. "Y'all ready for your table?" she asked, smiling at Emily.

Lucas recognized the woman. Mindy Hooper. She'd been a couple of years ahead of him in school. She hadn't changed much, though she seemed to have added thirty pounds or so, mostly below the waist.

Mindy greeted Wade with a "H'lo, Chief," then glanced automatically at Lucas. She nodded, then did a classic double take. "Lucas McBride?"

"Hello, Mindy. It's been a long time."

"No kidding. Where you been keepin' yourself, boy?"

"California, mostly."

"Well, it's good to see you," Mindy said firmly. "Never took much stock in all that gossip, myself. I just remember that you were always pretty nice to me when some people made fun of me 'cause I didn't have much money or anything.''

Lucas didn't quite know what to say. Mindy's words touched him, and he'd never been good at expressing that sort of emotion. "Er, uh, thanks," he muttered lamely.

Mindy nodded, turned and headed for a table. "Y'all follow me," she said over her shoulder.

Emily squeezed Lucas's hand as they walked toward their table. She must have sensed that he was feeling awkward. Lucas kept his gaze on her, ignoring the other people in the café. He'd always been pretty good at ignoring the people of this town.

He was beginning to think this lunch hadn't been such a bad idea, after all, when the situation took a sharp turn.

He looked up from his menu to find Rachel Jennings standing only a few feet away, staring at him with open consternation mirrored on her face.

RACHEL HAD NOT been particularly looking forward to having lunch with her uncle, but she'd felt obligated to accept when he called and extended the invitation. With the exception of her maternal grandmother, her father's younger brother was her only other relative in Honoria.

Rachel had never been close to Sam—she wasn't even particularly fond of him—but she saw no reason to avoid him entirely while she was in town. Once her grandmother moved to Carrollton, Rachel had no reason ever to return here. It might be years, if ever, before she would have occasion to see her uncle again.

They had agreed to meet at Cora's Café, a long time landmark of old, downtown Honoria. The café was lavishly decorated for the holidays with colored lights, tinsel, wreaths and ornament-covered trees. As she entered, Rachel wished she could feel some measure of holiday spirit herself.

Sam hadn't yet arrived when Rachel walked in. A slow-moving, kind-eyed waitress offered to show Rachel to a table for two, where she could wait comfortably. Rachel agreed.

She had gotten halfway across the busy room when she spotted Lucas sitting at a table with another man and a pretty blond woman. Rachel nearly stumbled.

Lucas looked up just as she saw him. Their gazes met and held. Rachel doubted her own expression was as unrevealing as Lucas's, but she made a massive effort to mask her emotions. She would have to pass right by his table to reach her own.

The woman with Lucas seemed to sense the sudden tension. She turned her head, following the direction of his gaze. Her blue eyes focused on Rachel's face, blankly at first, and then widened in apparent recognition.

Could this be Emily McBride? The shy, quiet little girl Rachel had seen occasionally from a distance while she and Lucas had been secretly involved? Emily had grown into a beautiful woman.

The waitress looked curiously over her shoulder, obviously wondering why Rachel had stopped. "This way, ma'am."

Rachel drew a deep breath, and started forward

again. She gestured to the waitress to indicate that she would seat herself in a moment. Something made her stop first at Lucas's table. Maybe she just needed to prove to him—and to herself—that she could see him and speak to him without falling apart. "Hello, Lucas."

Both men started to rise, but Rachel motioned for them to remain seated.

Lucas returned her greeting blandly, as if she were someone he hardly remembered. "Hello, Rachel. You remember my sister, Emily?"

Rachel nodded politely toward Emily. "We never formally met, but I remember. How are you, Emily?"

"I'm fine, thank you. This is my fiancé, Wade Davenport. Wade, this is Rachel Jennings. She's Jenny Holder's granddaughter."

Wade nodded. "I've met Mrs. Holder on several occasions."

"You're the chief of police, I've heard." Rachel extended her hand to the sleepy-eyed, roughly handsome man. "It's nice to meet you, Chief."

"Same here, Ms. Jennings. How is your grandmother? I understand she's been ill."

"Yes. Her health is getting too poor to allow her to live on her own much longer. I'm here to help her prepare to move to a retirement home in Carrollton."

"She'll be missed here. I know she has many friends in the community."

"She's lived here a long time."

There was a short, slightly awkward pause, and then Emily spoke up. "Will you join us for lunch, Rachel?"

"Thank you, but I'm meeting my uncle for lunch."

Emily's smile faded. Lucas's eyes darkened. Even Wade Davenport looked suddenly grim. It was obvious to Rachel that Sam Jennings wasn't exactly popular with this group.

Feeling the need to say something else, Rachel offered tentatively, "I've heard that you and Chief Davenport are getting married soon, Emily. Congratulations to you both."

"Thank you." Emily seemed pleased by the polite overture. "We'll be married New Year's Eve."

Rachel glanced at Lucas. "Did you come home for your sister's wedding?"

There was another short, taut silence before Lucas shook his head. "I'm only here through Christmas. Emily's wedding will proceed nicely without the black sheep of the family there to cause a scandal."

Emily frowned, obviously displeased with Lucas's decision.

Rachel wondered why Lucas wouldn't stay for the wedding. If there was one thing she knew about him, it was that he cherished his little sister. He had as a young man, and she sensed that he still did.

He'd made it sound as though he was staying away to spare Emily the embarrassment of having him there. Was his motive for missing his sister's wedding really so noble?

"What the hell...?"

The outraged bellow practically echoed through the small café, causing several startled diners to jump and look quickly around.

Rachel turned. Her uncle stood close by, his eyes glittering, his usually florid face even redder than usual.

"Get away from that table, Rachel," he snarled, staring at Lucas. "Are you too young to remember the man who caused your brother's death?"

Emily inhaled sharply. "Have you forgotten what I told you about slandering my brother? Unless you want to be slapped with a lawsuit, I'd advise you to be quiet."

Both Wade and Lucas looked at Emily with such affectionate approval that Rachel was almost envious for a moment.

Ignoring Emily's threat, Jennings pointedly turned his back on the table. "Let's get out of here, Rachel. We'll eat someplace where the air isn't as polluted."

Rachel winced. Her uncle was embarrassing her with his boorish behavior.

"There's a table all the way across the room, Sam," she pointed out quietly. "We can take that one. There's no need to carry on this way."

"I'm not staying. Being in the same room with a murderer, and watching our so-called police chief fawning over him, takes away my appetite."

"That does it." Emily started to rise.

Wade restrained his fiancée with a hand on her arm. "Maybe you'd *better* leave, Jennings. You're getting real close to disturbing the peace in here."

"Yeah, threaten me and let McBride sit there smirking," Jennings sneered. "We got ourselves one hell of a police chief here, neighbors."

He turned disdainfully on one heel. "Come along, Rachel," he said as though she were a child.

She lifted her chin, finding his tone offensive. She had no intention of meekly following her uncle's orders. "You go on," she said coolly. "I've decided there are other things I need to do this afternoon."

Sam muttered something ugly beneath his breath and stalked toward the exit. Many of the diners were watching Rachel openly, waiting to see what she would do. Lucas's dark blue eyes, trained on her face, were completely unreadable to her.

She sighed. "I'm sorry," she said to all three of them. "My uncle was out of line. He shouldn't have behaved that way. I hope we haven't ruined your lunch."

"You're still welcome to join us, Rachel," Emily said, after tossing a scornful look at Sam's departing back.

"Thank you, but I've decided I'm not hungry. I think I'll go check on my grandmother."

She risked another quick glance at Lucas. He met her eyes steadily, still giving no outward clue to his feelings—but somehow she sensed he wasn't quite as calm as he appeared. Her uncle's words must have infuriated Lucas, and probably embarrassed him. But no one would know by looking at him. Lucas had made masking his feelings an art form.

"I'm sorry," she repeated, looking only at him this time. And then she turned and walked away with as much dignity as she could muster.

5

"ALL IN ALL," Wade said later that afternoon, "there just wasn't enough evidence to convict you."

Lucas tossed a thick file folder onto Wade's desk. "That's because I didn't kill Roger Jennings. As far as I know, Roger fell from those bluffs without any help from anyone."

Wade settled back into his chair and assumed what seemed to be a characteristic pose for him—elbows on the arms of his chair, fingers steepled in front of him. "He was on McBride land. You and he had a public history of animosity. Several people around town heard you threaten each other."

"Roger and I made no secret of our mutual dislike. He was a jerk—and he believed all the garbage his family ever told him about the McBrides."

"He must have really hated it that you were in love with his sister."

For several long, tense moments, there was no sound in Wade's office except the ticking of the old cuckoo clock on the wall. Lucas stared at Wade's unrevealing expression. Finally he said, "You didn't read that in Packer's file."

"No."

"Did Emily say something?" Had his sister been more perceptive as a child than he'd realized?

"No. I don't think she knows."

"Then what the hell makes you think I was in love with Rachel Jennings?"

"Just a hunch I got, watching the two of you together in the café."

Hell. What was a cop of this caliber doing in a sleepy little burg like Honoria?

Wade gave him another moment, then prodded, "Roger must have been adamantly opposed to having you involved with his sister. I'd imagine he'd have done just about anything to keep the two of you apart."

"Are you looking for motives, Chief? Because if you're trying to close Packer's old case by pinning it on me…"

"I told you, I have no reason to believe you killed Roger Jennings. I'm just trying to understand what was going on around here fifteen years ago…and why Jennings ended up crumpled at the foot of a bluff on McBride land."

"I didn't push him. I didn't see him fall. As far as I know, it was an accident. It was dark, he took a wrong turn on the path. Maybe he'd been drinking."

"The autopsy ruled that out. He was sober."

Lucas nodded. "But it was dark. There was no moon that night. Roger was in a temper. Maybe he wasn't being careful and just walked off the path and into thin air."

It was the only explanation Lucas could come up with fifteen years ago…it was still the only one he had now. Nothing he'd seen in Packer's files even hinted that anyone else could have been involved. Of course, Packer hadn't bothered to look for other suspects. He'd have been quite happy to lock Lucas up for life...and if it hadn't been for Lizzie Carpenter, he might well have done so.

"He was in a temper, was he? Something you'd said?"

Lucas didn't answer.

"Did Roger forbid you and Rachel to see each other?"

"He had no right to 'forbid' either Rachel or me to do anything," Lucas refuted automatically.

"As I'm sure you must have told him."

"Yes."

"And Rachel? Did she tell him the same thing?"

"I would assume so."

"He probably considered himself the head of his household. His father deserted the family years earlier, his mother was known for being moody and depressive, his sister was several years younger. When he found out that something was going on between his kid sister and a man he'd been programmed to hate, he must have tried to put an end to it. I can't see you meekly agreeing to that."

"I didn't push him off that bluff," Lucas repeated flatly. "No matter what he said, he couldn't have kept me from seeing Rachel."

"How did Rachel react to her brother's interference? Was she as confident as you that Roger couldn't keep you apart? Or was she afraid that he *could*?"

"I don't know what you..."

"I don't suppose Rachel knew about your involvement with Lizzie Carpenter. Rachel might have thought Roger was the only obstacle between you."

Lucas stood so abruptly his chair clattered on the uncarpeted floor, teetering precariously on its back legs before steadying. "Are you implying that *Rachel...?*"

Wade held up his hands and cut in quickly. "I'm not implying anything. Just throwing out a few questions Packer apparently didn't ask."

Lucas shook his head. "Packer didn't know Rachel and I had been seeing each other. No one knew. And if you think Rachel had anything to do with Roger's death, you're not nearly as good a cop as I was beginning to think you are."

"You're the one who wanted to reopen the old case file," Wade pointed out. "I'm just asking the questions I might have asked if I'd been in charge of the investigation."

"Just be glad you weren't. Because if you'd started trying to pin something like this on Rachel..."

"What would you have done, Lucas? Pushed me off a cliff to protect her?"

Lucas slammed both hands down on Wade's desk and glared directly into his future brother-in-law's eyes. "I did *not* kill Roger Jennings. And neither did Rachel."

"So who did?"

"I don't know!"

"Just an accident?"

Lucas straightened, chagrined by his momentary loss of control. "I don't know," he repeated more quietly.

"You came back here because you heard about

the break-in at Emily's house. You thought it had something to do with Roger's death. I want to know what the connection was."

"I don't know what you're talking about."

"You asked me very specifically what was taken in the break-in. You seemed particularly interested in the bracelet she was wearing. Why?"

Lucas looked pointedly at his watch. "I have to go. Thanks for letting me look through the files."

Wade stood slowly, and his usual affable, innocuous expression had hardened into one of steely determination. "If Emily is in some sort of danger, I have as much right to protect her as you do—more even. I want to know what's going on, Lucas."

"If I thought there was anything you needed to know, I would tell you. As far as I can tell, Roger took a tumble all by himself fifteen years ago, and Emily was the victim of a crime ring operated by a couple of bored teenagers."

"Damn it, McBride..."

The outdated intercom on Wade's desk crackled. "I hate to interrupt, Chief, but Martha Godwin's on line two and she insists on talking to you. She claims the mailman peeked up her skirt while she was bent over her flower bed, and she wants you to arrest him."

Lucas pictured the scrawny, dried-up woman he'd known fifteen years ago. Martha Godwin had to be pushing seventy now. His mouth quirked. "You've obviously got a serious situation brewing here. I'll clear out and let you get to it. And be careful out there. It's a real jungle."

He stepped out of the office and closed the door on Wade's mild obscenity.

RACHEL SHIVERED as she stepped out of her grandmother's kitchen door into the backyard. It wasn't bitterly cold, but the heavy gray clouds rolling in from the west made it seem colder. It was supposed to rain later.

It had been raining the night Lucas left Honoria.

"Here, boy," she said, rattling dry dog food against the sides of the stainless-steel bowl in her right hand. "Want your dinner?"

"I've already eaten, thanks."

Lucas stepped out of the shadows at the same moment the dog bowl fell from Rachel's suddenly nerveless fingers. Kibble scattered on the ground at her feet. A hungry mutt of indeterminate heritage appeared to start gulping it down.

Rachel stepped out of the way before Gomer could mistake her shoelaces for dessert. "Are you *trying* to give me a heart attack before Christmas?" she asked Lucas irritably. "Can't you just pick up the phone like other people?"

"I've never been quite like other people."

She couldn't help smiling a little at that. She pushed her hands into the pockets of the oversized black cardigan she wore over a red tunic and black leggings. "What are you doing here?"

Instead of answering, Lucas nodded toward the noisily eating dog. "I take it your grandmother didn't get the mutt for protection."

"Actually, she did. Unfortunately, she forgot to tell him that she wants him to bark at people, not at cats and squirrels."

Rachel paused to clear her throat, then asked again, "Why are you here, Lucas? After the scene my uncle caused in the café, I'd have thought you'd want to stay away from the Jennings family."

"I always had trouble staying away from one member of it."

She didn't know what to say to that. She didn't like the way heat rushed into her cheeks, making her blush like the flustered teenager she'd once been around him.

Lucas shifted his weight. "Is your grandmother in bed?"

"Yes. She turns in early. Actually, she spends more time in bed than out these days."

"Will you go for a drive with me?"

Rachel wasn't sure she'd heard him correctly. "You want to go for a drive? Now?"

"Yes."

"Where?"

"Anywhere. Someplace where we can talk."

Going off in a car alone with Lucas sounded like a really bad idea to Rachel. So why was she even considering it?

"I don't..."

"Does your grandmother need you here?"

"No. As I said, she's sleeping. But..."

"You said you weren't afraid of me," Lucas reminded her.

"What do you want to talk to me about?" she hedged.

Lucas exhaled impatiently, and took a step back from her. "Look, if you don't want to go, just say so."

He sounded so much like the impatient, temperamental young man she'd known that her heart ached. He was already moving away. He had too much pride to beg her to go with him—and she wouldn't have wanted Lucas to beg, anyway.

"Lucas," she called out impulsively.

Without pausing, he looked over his shoulder. "What?"

"Will you wait until I get my purse?"

He stopped. "Yeah."

She was probably being an idiot—but there was nothing new about that where Lucas McBride was concerned.

"I'll be right back."

He crossed his arms over his chest and leaned against the trunk of the massive oak that shaded her grandmother's backyard in the summer. "Take your time," he said, patient now that he had the answer he wanted.

Rachel took less than ten minutes. Any longer, and she probably would have talked herself out of this impulsive behavior.

Fifteen years ago, Lucas had driven a battered old pickup truck. He'd bought it with the money he'd earned working at a series of odd jobs from the time he was twelve years old.

The sleek black sports car he drove now was a lot different from that old truck. She studied the vehicle's interior while Lucas walked around to his side after closing her door for her. The instrument panel was framed in glossy hardwood, and the stereo system was fancier than the one she had in her apartment in Atlanta.

"Nice car," she said as Lucas slid behind the

wheel. She needed to say something—being closed into the small, cozy space with him had made her heart suddenly start to trip in a manner that threatened her hard-won composure.

"I rented it at the Atlanta airport. It's a lot like the one I drive in California." He started the engine. It purred like a powerful jungle cat.

Rachel fastened her seat belt.

An oldies station was playing on the radio. The song was one Rachel and Lucas had listened to on his portable radio during those stolen afternoons at the bluff. She winced, and tried to keep her thoughts focused on the present.

"What do you do? For a living, I mean," she asked in a lame attempt to keep the conversation moving.

Lucas shrugged. "I play around with computers."

"And you live in California?"

"Most of the time."

For someone who'd wanted to talk, he wasn't being overly communicative. "You, er, haven't married?"

"No. Have you?"

"No."

She'd been engaged—very briefly. A few years ago she'd impulsively accepted a proposal to ease the loneliness inside her, but she'd known almost immediately that she couldn't go through with it. She hadn't been waiting for Lucas, of course, she assured herself. She just hadn't yet found anyone who could compete with her memories of the time she'd spent with him.

She said none of that now, of course.

Lucas drove past the Honoria city limits and kept going. Rachel leaned her head against the high back of her seat and left their destination in his hands. For now.

She still couldn't quite believe she was doing this. A few days ago, when she'd come to Honoria, she hadn't even expected to see Lucas. In fact, she'd even gone out of her way before coming here to make sure Lucas hadn't been seen or heard from since he'd left on that rainy night fifteen years ago.

If anyone had told her that not only would she see Lucas, she would slip out of her grandmother's house to go for a moonlight ride with him, just as she'd done as a teenager, she'd have laughed herself silly. All these years, she'd told herself she never wanted to see Lucas again. That she would never forgive him for the way he'd hurt her. And now here she was, tagging along with him again just because he'd asked her to. Unable to turn him away, even though he hadn't been particularly friendly to her since they'd run into each other again.

What was the hold this man had always had over her? And what would it take for her to break it once and for all?

"Run out of innocuous questions?" he murmured when they'd ridden several miles in silence. "We could always talk about the weather."

She turned her head to look at him. "Did you only want me to come along so you continue to be snide to me?"

"Am I being snide?"

"Yes."

"Sorry."

"No, you're not."

He glanced at her, the passing streetlights throwing intriguing shadows across his face. "I didn't think you would come tonight."

"Then why did you ask me?"

"Because I wanted you to," he answered after a moment.

She turned to look out her side window, hiding her face from him. "I probably shouldn't have come. I've worked very hard to forget the past."

"I haven't forgotten any of it."

She almost winced. "Emily's fiancé seemed nice," she said, grasping the first "innocuous" topic that came to mind. "Tell me about him."

"He's a cop. A widower. He's got a kid—a boy named Clay. They're both crazy about Emily."

It wasn't easy making conversation with this man, but Rachel persisted. "Why aren't you staying for the wedding? Do you have to get back to work?"

"No. I just think it will be better for Emily if I'm not there."

"Emily doesn't seem to agree."

"Emily's thinking with her heart instead of her head. She'll understand later."

"Don't you want to see her wedding?"

She thought his hands tightened on the steering wheel. But all he said was, "She'll be married whether I'm there to watch or not."

"You didn't answer my question. Don't you want to be there?"

He phrased his answer carefully. "If I thought I could go without causing a stir or taking attention away from Emily, I probably would."

Rachel settled back into her seat, satisfied that she'd finally gotten an honest answer out of Lucas. She didn't know why that had been so important.

She almost groaned aloud when a new song started playing on the radio. Neil Diamond's "Hello, Again," which had been one of her favorites when she and Lucas were together. It still made her throat tighten every time she heard it.

She wished Lucas would change the station to something less evocative of the past. Country, maybe. Or rap. Anything but Neil Diamond.

Lucas nodded toward an all-night diner ahead. "How about some pie and coffee?"

"Yes, all right."

She didn't really want pie or coffee, but maybe being in a brightly lit, public place with other people around them would dispel the disturbing feeling of intimacy created by being alone in a quiet, darkened car with him while old love songs played on the radio. At least, she hoped it would.

LUCAS LOOKED across the table at Rachel and wondered what she was doing here with him. She toyed unenthusiastically with her pecan pie, avoiding his eyes. She looked as though she'd rather be anywhere but here.

So why had she come?

For that matter, he wasn't exactly sure why he had asked her.

He'd always been lousy at making small talk. He and Rachel had never had trouble talking in the past, but a lot had happened since then. He cleared his throat and tried to think of something to say.

Almost anything would be better than this strained silence.

When they weren't talking, it was far too easy—uncomfortably easy—for him to remember how they'd passed the time together on those long, lazy afternoons fifteen years ago.

"How do you like accounting?" he asked awkwardly, forcefully shoving memories of hungry, innocent kisses out of his mind. "I guess it gets pretty busy at the end of the year."

"I like it okay," she replied absently. "And, yes, it does…"

She stopped suddenly and frowned at him. "How did you know I'm an accountant?"

"You, er, must have mentioned it."

"No."

"Someone else, then."

She looked at him suspiciously. Lucas returned the look without expression. He had no intention of telling her that he'd kept tabs on her—just as he had his sister—during the past fifteen years. Rachel might be amazed at what could be learned by someone who knew his way around the Internet.

"Lucas…"

"How's your pie?"

She looked automatically at her plate. "It's fine."

"More coffee?" He signaled the waitress, pointing toward his nearly empty cup.

The efficient server had their cups refilled before Rachel could answer. "Y'all need anything else?"

Lucas shook his head. "Just the check."

The woman laid a slip of paper on the table beside Lucas's hand. "Merry Christmas," she said, sounding as though she was rather tired of the phrase.

Rachel pushed the rest of her pie away and reached for the steaming coffee. "Emily must be so pleased to have you home for Christmas, even if you aren't staying for the wedding."

Lucas swallowed the last bite of his chocolate pie. "Yeah, I guess."

"Have you seen any more of your family since you've been in town?"

"Bobbie and Caleb made a short visit Monday evening. The cousins will be arriving tomorrow—I think most of them are planning to stay through New Year's day."

"They're staying for the wedding, I suppose."

He didn't know why Rachel kept bringing up Emily's wedding. She seemed to disapprove of his plan to skip the ceremony. But surely she could understand why he thought it best to do so.

She'd said she'd tried to forget the past. He doubted that she'd really forgotten the way people had whispered about him before he'd left town.

From the time Lucas was a kid, he'd given the bored gossips of Honoria plenty to gab about. His secret meetings with Rachel would really have had their jaws flapping—which was the reason he'd been so careful to keep those meetings secret.

"Are you looking forward to seeing your cousins again?"

He grimaced. "Not particularly. Basically, they're like strangers to me. They're all younger than I am—I didn't know them very well even before I left town."

"The few cousins I have are scattered around the

country. I rarely see them." Rachel sounded a bit wistful.

"At least you don't have to spend Christmas trying to make conversation with them." Lucas dreaded that.

Rachel shook off her introspective mood and forced a smile. "Have you finished your Christmas shopping?"

Lucas frowned. "I...er..."

"You haven't done any?" She lifted an eyebrow.

"I'm not very good at that sort of thing," he admitted.

"Surely you'll want to get something for Emily. And you'll probably want to get her a wedding gift, too."

"A, uh, wedding gift," he repeated blankly. Did she mean something like a toaster? Emily probably already had a toaster.

"And you'll want to get a gift for Chief Davenport's son—he's about to be your nephew, of course. Maybe something for your aunt and uncle."

Rachel stopped suddenly and flushed. "Sorry. It's none of my business who you do or do not buy Christmas gifts for. I'm hardly an expert on family Christmases. I usually have dinner with my mother on Christmas Eve, then spend Christmas Day watching Jimmy Stewart and Bing Crosby movies and eating myself into a stupor. What do *you* usually do on Christmas?"

He shrugged. "I usually work. It's the one day I can almost guarantee I won't be interrupted."

Rachel studied him across the table. "I don't

know which of our stories is more pathetic," she murmured.

Lucas stood abruptly and tossed some bills on the table. "Let's go."

Rachel looked a bit startled, but she rose obligingly. "I was finished, anyway."

Lucas didn't bother to reply as he led her out of the diner and into the cool, damp night air.

6

IT BEGAN TO RAIN just as Lucas drove out of the diner's parking lot. The rain fell gently against the roof of the car, a soft, steady background to the oldies still playing on the radio. The sound of the rain took Rachel back to that Saturday afternoon in the rock house. She'd been so happy then. So desperately in love.

So young.

She risked a sideways look at Lucas. Did he remember that day? He seemed so different from the hot-tempered, passionate, reckless young man she'd known before. Now he was more stern. Quiet. So self-contained, she found it almost impossible to read his expressions.

And yet...he was still Lucas. And, in some ways, she still felt as though she knew him very well.

She reminded herself that she'd once thought she'd known him better than anyone else in the world. And yet he'd hurt her in a way she'd been totally unprepared to handle.

She'd been so damned young.

When Lucas turned off the main road and onto the country lane that led to McBride land, Rachel frowned. This was the road that ended at the bluffs. Why was Lucas driving this way?

If he thought they were going to indulge in the

old-fashioned "parking" they'd spent so much time here doing as teenagers, then she intended to firmly let him know that wasn't going to happen. Tonight, or ever again. Or, at least, she hoped that's what she'd find the willpower to say to him, she thought, remembering just how exciting and delicious those interludes had once been.

He stopped the car at the gate that prevented them from driving all the way to the end of the lane. "I didn't know this gate was here."

"I've climbed over it twice now," Rachel confessed.

"My father must have installed it. He was never particularly encouraging to visitors, anyway."

"For some reason, there was a steady stream of sightseers to the bluffs after you left. You'd be surprised how many people wanted to see the place where my brother died." She heard the undertone of bitterness in her voice, but couldn't seem to do anything about it.

Lucas looked straight ahead, through the rain-splattered windshield. "You'd think people would have better things to do with their time."

"Yes." Rachel twisted her fingers in her lap, remembering the inquisitive looks. The whispers. The blatantly intrusive questions.

"There are a couple of things I want to ask you, Rachel. I'm not sure how to begin."

His hesitation seemed uncharacteristic. She gripped her hands more tightly together. "Just ask."

"How much did Roger talk to you in the days before he died?"

Watching Lucas as closely as she could in the

darkness, Rachel chose her words carefully. "Roger and I never talked much. You knew we weren't particularly close. We tended to argue, because he wanted to tell me what to do and I didn't like it when he did."

"Did he say anything about your father's disappearance?"

"That was something that was *never* mentioned in my house," Rachel answered flatly, wondering where Lucas's questions were leading. "My mother became hysterical every time she heard my father's name. Roger and I learned very young to avoid speaking of him."

"Roger never said anything to you about finding a gold bracelet?"

Rachel was growing more confused with each question. "No. Why?"

Instead of answering, Lucas asked yet another question. "Did Roger say anything to you about your involvement with me?"

Rachel froze. "Roger didn't know I was seeing you. I made very sure he never found out. He'd have been furious if he knew. He hated you."

"He made that very clear when he told me he would kill me if I ever saw you again."

Rachel couldn't say anything for several minutes. "Roger found out about us?"

"Yes."

"When?"

"He came to me the day after you and I last saw each other. He told me then to stay away from you."

"He didn't say anything to me. I thought he was

acting even surlier than usual, but...why didn't he say anything?''

"He probably thought you'd be even more determined to see me if he tried to forbid you. So he came to me, instead, hoping to scare me off."

"He didn't know you very well, did he?"

"He didn't know me at all. He knew only that I was a McBride. And that's all he cared to know."

Rachel's' hands were beginning to ache, but she couldn't seem to loosen her grip. "I...always wondered what Roger was doing here that night. Do you think he was watching for me? Spying to see if I was going to meet you?"

Lucas shot her a quick, searching look. "Some people said I lured him here so I could push him off the bluffs."

"I know what some people said."

His fingers flexed on the steering wheel. "You didn't believe them?"

"If there had been one shred of evidence against you, Chief Packer would have put you behind bars. And, besides, you weren't even here that night."

Roger had most definitely been in the wrong place at the wrong time, Rachel thought sadly. If he'd been trying to catch Lucas slipping around to meet someone, he should have been watching Lizzie Carpenter's house.

Lucas didn't seem particularly satisfied with Rachel's answer. Without moving, he watched the rain, his thoughts seeming very far away.

Rachel was trying to think of something to say to break the silence when Lucas finally spoke again. "You never told your mother about us?"

Her mother would have totally freaked out. Jane had bitterly disliked all McBrides after her husband ran off with Lucas's stepmother.

"I never told anyone about us." Not her family, not her closest friends…no one.

While they were together, Lucas had been Rachel's cherished secret. The secrecy had made their relationship seem even more romantic and magical.

She'd sat in her classrooms, bored with the teachers' lectures, daydreaming about the day she and Lucas would surprise everyone by announcing their love for each other. Or maybe they would elope, she'd fantasized. They would return to Honoria as Mr. and Mrs. Lucas McBride, and all the girls would be so envious that quiet, shy, good-girl Rachel Jennings had caught the most exciting, daring, dangerous bad boy in town.

Had she really been that naive and foolish?

She had grown up fast the day she'd been told her brother was dead—and that the only reason Lucas hadn't been arrested for his murder was because he'd spent that fateful night in Lizzie Carpenter's bed.

And then he'd left town, without a word. He'd abandoned her at the lowest point of her young life, leaving her with a devastated, embittered mother and a secret that had become more tragic than romantic.

She could forgive him for most of the things he'd done—maybe she could even forgive him for Lizzie—but she still couldn't remember his leaving the way he had without being overwhelmed by a wave of betrayal.

Shouldn't she have gotten past that by now? It had been so long ago. They'd both gotten older. She wasn't sure, however, that she had gotten much wiser. If she had, why was she sitting here now with Lucas McBride?

Maybe a similar thought crossed his mind. He reached for the ignition and started the car. "It's getting late. I'll take you home."

Home. Rachel mulled the word over in her mind as he drove. Where *was* home? Certainly not her grandmother's house, though that was where she'd lived from the time her father had abandoned his family when she was only nine until she'd left for college nine years later. The functional, few-frills apartment she maintained in Atlanta had never really had the feel of "home." It was just a place to live.

"Home" wasn't a place, she'd always heard, but a feeling. Rachel had been waiting a long time to find a refuge to call home. She'd begun to wonder lately if she ever would.

Lucas had always had an uncanny ability to sense what she was thinking. "What's your life like in Atlanta?"

"Quiet," she answered after a moment. "Peaceful. I have a good job, a nice apartment, a few good friends."

"Is that all you want?"

Something about his question made her defensive. Okay, so maybe her life at thirty-three was much different from her daydreams at eighteen. But it wasn't all that bad. She had made her choices, and she was content with them, for the most part.

"It's all I want for now," she answered a bit shortly.

It was still raining when Lucas drove into the driveway of her grandmother's house.

"Hold on a minute," he said, reaching over the back of his seat into the tiny storage space behind. He pulled out an umbrella. "Sit tight, I'll come around."

"I can make a run for it," she protested, reaching for her door handle. "There's no need for you to get out."

"Stay," he said, and opened his door.

She didn't particularly liked being talked to like a trained pet. But she didn't move until Lucas opened her door and held the umbrella over her as she climbed out.

He looped his left arm around her shoulders, holding the umbrella over them both with his right hand. Rachel huddled into her jacket, telling herself Lucas had pulled her close only to ensure that she stayed dry.

She still wasn't sure why he'd invited her to accompany him this evening, but there'd been nothing in the least suggestive about his behavior. He'd treated her like an old friend he'd run into by chance. Which, she told herself quickly, was just fine with her.

He lowered the umbrella when they stepped under the small porch at her grandmother's front door. Rachel fumbled in her purse for the key. At least this time, she didn't have to crawl in through her bedroom window, as she'd had to do fifteen years ago, she thought wryly.

She looked up at him. "Thank you for the pie and coffee."

"Tomorrow is Christmas Eve."

He had a bewildering habit of replying in non sequiturs. It took her a moment to catch up. "Yes?"

"If I'm going to buy presents, I guess I'll have to do it in the morning."

"Probably," she agreed, somewhat amused by his grim tone. He looked as though he was planning a root canal.

"I could use some help. Will you go with me?"

"Er…" Caught off guard, she hesitated.

"I don't have anyone else to ask," he said simply.

Hardly the most flattering justification, but it was honest enough and innocuous enough to put Rachel more at ease. "Do you really think it's a good idea for us to be seen Christmas shopping together? Can you imagine the gossip? But then again, I guess there aren't that many people in town who know us…"

"After that scene in the café today? Don't kid yourself. Everyone in Honoria knows we're here now. And that you spoke politely to my sister and me before your uncle showed up."

"I suppose you're right," she admitted. "The gossip lines have probably been buzzing all afternoon."

"Still, I see no reason to give them any more material. I thought I'd drive to the mall over in Logan's Ridge to do my shopping. Chances are less likely there for us to run into anyone we know."

She couldn't help thinking about the past again. She and Lucas had always been so careful not to be seen together. They had known what a stir it would create if people knew they'd fallen for each other, despite their family history. How much more scandalous would it be if she were seen with him *now*?

"We could take our own cars," she said, the suggestion escaping her almost before she knew it. "Meet at the mall."

"That would be fine. How about just inside the main entrance at 10:00 a.m.?"

Rachel nodded. "All right. I'll see you then."

She had some shopping of her own to do, she rationalized. Even though all of it could have waited until after Christmas.

She turned toward the door. Lucas's hand on her arm compelled her to face him again.

"There's something I've been wanting to do since I saw you standing in that rock house Monday," he muttered.

Before she could ask what he meant, he covered her mouth in a hard, fierce kiss that nearly made her knees buckle.

Memories of the past evaporated in the heat of the present. Rachel was no longer a shy, inexperienced girl. And Lucas wasn't an eager, impulsive young man. The years had changed both of them.

But the chemistry between them was still there. Still so powerful it threatened to explode.

She was still clinging to Lucas's jacket when he finally drew away. One by one, she loosened her fingers, dropping her hands heavily to her sides.

She stared at him, her mind completely blank.

It took Lucas a few moments to speak. When he did, it was only to say, "I'll see you tomorrow."

He turned on one booted heel and walked away without bothering to use the umbrella. The cold rain must have soaked him through by the time he reached his car, but he didn't seem to notice. He threw the umbrella inside and climbed in after it.

Rachel didn't want him to see her watching him drive away. She turned quickly and opened the door, closing herself into her grandmother's house. And then she peeked through the filmy curtain over the diamond-shaped window in the door and watched until Lucas's taillights had disappeared from sight.

GOING TO THE MALL to help Lucas with his Christmas shopping was *not* a good idea, Rachel told herself as she tossed and turned in her bed Wednesday night. She was still trying to convince herself as she showered Thursday morning and dressed in a cheery Christmas sweater and a pair of black jeans. And even as she kissed her grandmother's cheek and went out to her car, she was cursing herself for a fool.

And as she drove through the crowded mall parking lot, looking in vain for a space, she admitted that she was also looking for an excuse to turn around and go home.

She finally found an opening at the farthest edge of the lot. She took it, to the annoyance of a man in a Cadillac who'd been trying to beat Rachel to the space.

"So much for Christmas spirit," she muttered as the guy flipped her a finger and drove on.

At least the rain had stopped. The sun was shining in a cloudless, winter-blue sky. It wasn't even cold enough that she had to wear a jacket over her warm sweater. She hurried toward the main entrance, wondering if Lucas would be waiting for her—or if he, too, had come to the conclusion that this was a really dumb idea.

A Salvation Army volunteer stood beside a bucket, ringing a bell and looking tired even though it was still early. Rachel stuffed a couple of bills into the bucket.

"Bless you. Merry Christmas."

Rachel smiled. "Merry Christmas to you, too."

And then she drew a deep breath and entered the mall.

For a moment, she was disoriented by the cacophony of noise, lights, glittering decorations and milling bodies. How would she ever find...?

A hand fell on her arm.

"Thank you for coming," Lucas said as he stepped in front of her, his black jacket, shirt and slacks a somber contrast to the colorful background.

Rachel didn't smile. "I almost didn't come."

"I know."

She grimaced. "You're claiming to know my thoughts now?'

"I know *you*."

He had known the girl. He didn't know the woman. But this wasn't the time to tell him, she thought as a shopper loaded down with packages jostled her.

Rachel tucked her purse more firmly beneath her arm. "Let's go."

Lucas nodded grimly. "Yeah. Let's get this over with."

Lucas's idea of shopping, Rachel soon discovered, was to enter a store, point to something, and say, "I'll take it."

In an electronics store, he bought Wade Davenport's son the newest, most sophisticated hand-held electronic game on the market. The cost nearly made Rachel choke.

"That's pretty fancy for a nine-year-old boy," she murmured. "Are you sure it isn't too much?"

He shrugged. "The programs are upgradable. They range from his age level to adult. It should do him for several years."

"It's expensive."

Lucas's mouth quirked. "I've only got one nephew. At the moment."

After paying for the game, he led her to a sporting-goods store. "Emily said Wade likes to fish," he commented. He nabbed a busy salesclerk. "Got anything new for fly fishermen?"

The clerk took one look at Lucas and led him to an array of expensive fishing accessories.

Fifteen minutes later, Lucas turned to Rachel. "Now for Emily."

"Lead the way," she murmured, her tone wry.

He walked into a jewelry store, pointed to a pair of diamond solitaire earrings and said, "I'd like to see those, please."

The first pair he was shown didn't please him. The second pair did. "These will be fine. Do you gift wrap?"

Rachel glanced at all the busy shoppers scurrying around them, looks of harried desperation on their faces as they tried to find something for everyone on their lists. Lucas had been shopping for just over an hour—most of that time spent standing in line—and he'd already accomplished his goals.

"I thought I'd pick up a nice bottle of wine for Bobbie and Caleb," he said to Rachel, tucking Emily's earrings into the bigger bag that held his other gifts. "I'll send Emily and Wade a wedding gift later."

She planted her hands on her hips. "Is there anything else you need me to help you with?" she asked very politely.

He lifted an eyebrow. "Is something wrong?"

"You knew exactly what you wanted to buy everyone on your list. You didn't need my help. Why did you want me here?"

He returned her look blandly. "I don't like to shop alone."

Two children in a hurry for a last-minute visit with the mall Santa pushed past Rachel, followed closely by their weary mother. Still looking at Lucas, Rachel ignored them. "Do you have anything else to buy?"

"No. I think I've fulfilled all my Christmas obligations."

"Then let's have lunch. I skipped breakfast and I'm hungry. And by the way," she added, thinking of how casually he'd just spent a rather sizeable chunk of money, "you're buying."

He laughed. The rusty sound seemed to surprise him almost as it did her. "You're on."

Lucas refused to eat at the food court or one of the crowded chain restaurants in the mall. They chose, instead, to drive their separate vehicles the short distance to a locally-owned Italian restaurant that had been in business for many years. Judging from the number of cars in the lot, it was still quite popular. And it was still a bit early for the real lunch-time rush.

"There will be a twenty-minute wait for a table," a perky young hostess informed them.

Lucas nodded. "We'll wait in the bar."

Christmas carols played softly from hidden speakers as Rachel and Lucas sat at a tiny table. The bartender had recommended his special hot cider in honor of the holiday, so they had decided to try it. Rachel was glad she did as she sipped the rich, steaming brew. "This is delicious."

"It's good."

"Your family will probably have a huge dinner tonight."

"Emily was already cooking when I left. If everyone else brings as much, there will be enough food for most of Honoria."

"And what are your plans for tomorrow?"

"Wade and Clay are staying over tonight. Emily wants to see Clay open his gifts from Santa Claus and then we'll have a big Christmas breakfast. I offered to clear out tonight so it would just be the three of them in the morning, but Emily wouldn't hear of it. She claims she needs me there as a chaperone. My sister," he added ruefully, "inherited her full share of the McBride obstinacy."

"After being separated from you for so long, I'm sure she wants to spend as much time with you as possible before you leave again."

"That's what she says."

Rachel searched his face. "Why do you find that so surprising?"

"Emily has every reason to resent the hell out of me for leaving the way I did. Our father was a cold son of a bitch who was incapable of showing her any real affection. All the old meddlers in town loved to rehash the stories about Nadine's running around, about the fights I got into, and about the speculation that I'd had something to do with Roger's death. After I left, there were apparently other scandals in the McBride family, so Emily bore the brunt of the gossip."

"From what I've heard, the townspeople are very fond of Emily, for the most part—despite her McBride blood."

Lucas nodded. "She's made a place for herself. I'm afraid she's had to swallow her pride a few times to stay in the town's good graces, but she doesn't seem to regret her choices. And she tells me she's learning to take up for herself when it's necessary."

Rachel twisted her cider mug between her hands. "When are you going back to California?"

He shrugged. "I promised to stay through Christmas. I'll probably clear out first thing on the twenty-sixth. Emily has a lot to do to get ready for her wedding next week, even though she's keeping it simple. I don't want to be in her way."

"Somehow I don't think she would see you as an inconvenience," Rachel murmured, remembering the way Emily had looked at her brother.

Lucas stared at his mug. "How long are *you* going to be in town?"

"It will probably take another week for me to get Grandmother's affairs in order."

"Sir? Ma'am? Your table is ready."

In response to the hostess's summons, Rachel and Lucas stood and followed her into the dining room, to a nicely secluded table for two. They glanced at the menu, placed their orders, then studied each other until their meals arrived.

"You haven't mentioned what you and your grandmother are doing for the holiday," Lucas said.

"After dinner—which I'm going to cook for us— my grandmother wants me to take her to her church for a candlelight service. She hasn't missed one in almost fifty years. She's very aware that this will be the last one she'll attend here."

"You won't be seeing your mother for Christmas?"

"Mother won't come back to Honoria. We decided to postpone our holiday dinner until New Year's day. She's spending this evening with a couple of single friends from her widow's support group."

Lucas didn't say anything, but Rachel felt a need to explain, anyway. "Mother tells everyone her husband died twenty-four years ago. As far as she's concerned, of course, he did."

Lucas frowned down at his plate. "No one has heard from your father since he ran off with my stepmother? He's never made any contact with anyone?"

She shook her head. "He never even tried to claim the money he left in savings accounts and other investments. If he ever knew his son had died, he made no effort to contact us. For all I know, he may be dead. Mother has every right to claim widowhood, if that makes her more comfortable."

"Yes, she does. Er...your brother had a theory of his own about why your father disappeared."

Rachel didn't know what Lucas was talking about. "What do you mean?"

"He decided that my father killed Al and Nadine and hid the bodies, then told everyone they'd run off together."

7

Rachel realized that her jaw had dropped. She closed her mouth, then shook her head. "That's insane. What makes you think Roger believed such a thing?"

"He told me. The night he ordered me to stop seeing you. He said he wouldn't allow his sister to be involved with the stepson of a whore and the son of a murderer. When I asked what the hell he was talking about, he told me his crazy theory. And then he pulled out what he claimed was proof that he was right."

She could hardly believe what she was hearing. "What kind of proof?"

"A gold bracelet. It was covered in dirt and dried mud, but I recognized it. It had belonged to Nadine. She never took it off."

"Where did Roger find Nadine's bracelet?"

"He said he'd been walking in the woods behind the rock house—which is where he claimed your father and my stepmother used to secretly meet. He claimed his dog dug up the bracelet. From that evidence, he concluded that Nadine and Al were buried somewhere in those woods."

"This is crazy," Rachel murmured, shaking her head in dazed disbelief. "I know Roger had a hard time accepting our father's disappearance, but how could he have come up with this ridiculous theory?"

"He refused to accept that Al would abandon his children for Nadine. It was easier for him to believe that your father was dead than to admit Al cared so little about the two of you that he would simply disappear from your lives forever."

"I didn't like admitting it, either," Rachel replied. "And I doubt that Emily likes knowing that her mother ran off when she was just a baby. But this..."

Lucas nodded grimly. "That's pretty much the way I reacted when Roger threw this tale at me. I thought he'd lost his mind. I told him my father was a bastard, but he wasn't a murderer. My father never cared enough about anyone to be driven to that point."

"Nadine must have dropped the bracelet by accident. Finding it in those woods is no proof of anything."

"That's what I told Roger."

"And what did he say?"

"That he had more proof."

"What?"

Lucas shook his head. "He wouldn't tell me. He said I would believe him when he found..."

"When he found what?" Rachel prompted.

"The bodies."

She pushed her plate away, leaving her lunch half-finished. "That's what he was doing in your woods that night? Looking for my father's body?"

"Either that or hoping to catch you meeting me there so he could force a confrontation. I don't know."

Scrubbing a hand over her face, Rachel sighed. "Why did you tell me all this?"

"Because I thought you had a right to know. And because…"

Again, he hesitated. Again, Rachel prodded. "What?"

"A couple of months ago, someone broke into Emily's house. She walked in and was knocked unconscious. When she woke up, she found her room had been ransacked and some of her jewelry was missing—including the bracelet she was wearing when she entered the house."

Rachel was horrified. She'd been told there'd been a series of break-ins around Honoria, but she hadn't heard about the attack on Emily. "Is that why you came back? Because you heard about the break-in and you wanted to make sure Emily was all right?"

"The bracelet taken from her wrist was the one Roger found in the woods. Emily had discovered where I'd stashed it before I left. I didn't realize she had found it until I read in a newspaper article that a gold bracelet belonging to her mother had been stolen. As far as I knew, Nadine had left no other gold bracelet behind—and even if she had, my father got rid of everything that had belonged to Nadine. He didn't save *anything* for Emily. It bothered me that nothing else of consequence was taken. I couldn't help wondering if there was any connection between that bracelet and the attack on Emily."

"What connection could there possibly have been?"

Looking a bit sheepish, Lucas shrugged. "I

haven't found any reason not to believe Emily was simply in the wrong place at the wrong time."

Rachel linked her hands in her lap beneath the table, gripping her napkin between them. "Even if the bracelet was evidence that Nadine had been…killed, the only person who would want the evidence hidden—your father—was already dead when Emily was attacked."

Lucas nodded, though his frown only deepened.

"Unless, of course," Rachel murmured, carried away for a moment by imagination, "someone else had reason to want that bracelet to remain hidden. Someone who took advantage of the break-ins to target Emily specifically to get the bracelet."

Lucas grimaced. "Doesn't sound very likely, does it?"

"That's what you thought? That Emily was attacked just so someone could take her mother's bracelet from her?"

"I don't know what I thought. But it seemed like a good time to come back and check on her. I, er, didn't know you'd be here."

Rachel pleated her napkin. "Are you sorry now that you came back?"

After a moment, he answered simply, "No."

She bit her lip.

"Are *you* sorry I came back?"

She didn't know how to answer that one. "I…"

Lucas gave a dry, humorless chuckle. "Never mind. Do you want dessert?"

"No, thank you. I'd better go check on my grandmother."

He nodded. "Thank you for helping me with my shopping."

"I'm not sure I was much help, but you're welcome, anyway."

Though the check had not yet arrived, the bills Lucas tossed on the table were more than sufficient to pay for their meals. "I'll walk you to your car."

The parking lot was even more crowded now than before, and traffic was heavy on the streets. But Rachel wasn't aware of anyone except the tall, dark man walking at her side.

She unlocked her car door, then looked up at him. "Lunch was very…enlightening. Thank you for telling me the things Roger said to you. I suppose you answered some questions for me."

"And provoked a few new ones, I'm certain."

"Yes."

Lucas glanced at the street. "There's a lot of traffic. Drive carefully."

"I will." She opened her door, then hesitated. Without looking at him, she asked, "Will I see you again before you leave?"

"You know where to find me. If you want to find me."

She looked up at him. "You hurt me very badly, Lucas. It took me a long time to get over you."

A muscle twitched in his jaw. "How long *did* it take?" he asked after a moment.

Fifteen years and counting, she almost answered. But she wasn't prepared to be quite *that* honest. "Too long," she said quietly.

He stepped back. "Goodbye, Rachel."

At least he'd said it this time. She nodded mutely and climbed into her car, made clumsy by her haste and the thin film of tears that had suddenly appeared in her eyes.

CALEB AND BOBBIE McBride's house was filled almost to the rafters with people. And all of them seemed to be talking at once.

Lucas, who'd admittedly been somewhat of a loner for the past fifteen years, attending social occasions only when absolutely necessary, was having a rather difficult time keeping up with everything going on around him.

His relatives had all been told he would be there, so they greeted him with more curiosity than surprise. His Aunt Bobbie, the hostess for the evening, took it upon herself to introduce Lucas back into the family. Holding his arm in a grip that felt more restraining than supportive, she propelled him around the room.

"You remember my daughter, Tara, of course," she said in her booming, schoolteacher's voice.

Lucas nodded pleasantly to his delicately pretty cousin, hoping he wasn't expected to kiss her or anything. He told himself he hardly remembered her—though he was sure her hair had been blond last time he'd seen her, rather than the flattering dark red it was now. "Nice to see you again, Tara."

She answered with a touch of the shyness he remembered. "Hello, Lucas. I'd like you to meet my husband, Blake Fox."

Blake Fox was golden-blond with bright, sharp blue eyes. He wore a loose-fitting blue shirt, suspenders, and pleated gray slacks that could have come from the wardrobe of an old Cary Grant movie. An eccentric type, obviously, Lucas mused, remembering that Emily had told him Fox was a private investigator.

"So you're the prodigal son I've heard so much

about," Blake said, taking Lucas's hand in a firm grip.

"I'm more often referred to as the black sheep of the family," Lucas drawled.

"No, that's *my* title," a well-built blonde murmured as she moved close to Lucas's side. "Let's keep the facts straight, cuz."

Lucas didn't have to be told who this was. "Well, if it isn't the beauty queen. Where's your tiara, Savannah?"

"Still as obnoxious as ever, I see." She didn't wait for Lucas to decide how to greet her, but rose on tiptoes to lightly kiss his cheek. "Welcome back, Lucas."

"Thanks."

It was possible, Lucas decided, that Savannah was no longer the spoiled, shallow cheerleader he'd remembered, just as he had outgrown his smart mouth and fiery temper. She was, however, as stunningly attractive as ever.

She drew a dark-haired, dark-eyed man to her side. "This is my husband, Kit Pace."

Lucas shook the man's hand. "Christopher Pace. I've read and enjoyed several of your books."

"Thank you. It's nice to finally have a chance to meet you. I've heard a bit about you."

Responding to Pace's wry tone, Lucas chuckled. "I imagine you have," he muttered, glancing at the stern-faced woman hovering nearby. She had positioned herself rather protectively between Lucas and a couple of teenagers Lucas assumed to be Savannah's twins. "Hello, Ernestine."

His widowed aunt-by-marriage nodded stiffly. "Lucas. What brings you back to Honoria? We noticed you didn't make it back for your father's funeral last spring."

Savannah rolled her eyes. "Mother…"

Ernestine exhaled impatiently. "All right, I won't say anything more. I just can't help wondering what he's after, showing up now after all these years."

"My inheritance, of course," Lucas answered, his voice hard. "I'm here to claim my share of the McBride legacy."

Since the McBride legacy had been one of scandal rather than fortune, Ernestine was left with very little to say in response.

Savannah quickly introduced Lucas to her twins, Miranda and Michael. Not knowing what to say to the wide-eyed adolescents, Lucas nodded and murmured something he hoped was sufficient.

Bobbie towed him then to another corner of the room where her sons, Trevor and Trent, waited. Trevor, married and the father of a small son, had a political appointment of some sort in Washington, D.C. Lucas thought his cousin looked very much the young politician with his GQ clothes and expensive haircut, but he seemed pleasant enough when he shook Lucas's hand and introduced his pregnant, picture-perfect wife.

Trent, the youngest of the McBride cousins at twenty-two, was a senior at the Air Force academy, as was evident from his military haircut and board-straight posture.

"I remember you," he said, shaking Lucas's hand. "You taught me to ride my bike."

"I did?" Lucas frowned. "Are you sure?"

Trent chuckled. "Yeah. Dad had about given up

because I was so afraid of falling that I screamed every time he let go of the bike. You waited until he went inside, then you plopped me down on the seat, pointed me downhill and let go. I was too intimidated by you to argue and too afraid of falling to ignore the instructions you yelled after me. By the time I got to the bottom of the hill, I was balancing like a pro."

Lucas sort of remembered now. It was just a bit hard to reconcile his memory of a tearful, tow-headed little boy with this tall, self-assured young man.

Family. Funny how he was beginning to feel a part of this one again, after spending so many years on his own.

A small hand slipped suddenly into Lucas's. He looked down to find Clay Davenport gazing up at him.

"I asked Santa for a new bike for Christmas," the boy reminded him eagerly. "Will you help *me* ride it if I get one, Uncle Lucas?"

Rather touched by the boy's gesture, Lucas nodded. "Sure, kid. But you have to promise to wear a helmet every time you ride."

"Even on hot days?" Clay asked, wrinkling his nose.

"Every single time," Lucas replied firmly. "Riding a bike without a helmet is totally uncool."

Clay squared his shoulders, making an effort to look as "cool" as possible, for a snub-nosed eight-year-old. "I'll wear a helmet all the time, Uncle Lucas. I promise."

He nodded in satisfaction. "Good."

"Once again," Wade murmured, placing his

hands on his son's shoulders, "you're being pretty confident that Santa's going to bring you a bike."

Clay smiled winningly. "I've been *very* good this year."

Wade chuckled and ruffled the boy's hair. "We'll see if Santa agrees."

"I imagine everyone's getting hungry," Bobbie announced, clapping her hands for attention. "Let's get the food out so we can eat."

Having now met and been greeted by everyone, Lucas found himself being treated with the same casual warmth as the others—almost as if it hadn't been fifteen years since he'd last joined them for Christmas dinner. But even as he mingled with his family, he found himself thinking of Rachel, and wondering what it would be like if she were here with him at the McBride family gathering.

HER STRENGTH drained from the exertion of attending the church candlelight service, Rachel's grandmother went to bed almost immediately after they returned home. Rachel found herself sitting alone in the quiet house with several hours of Christmas Eve still lying ahead of her.

She tried for a while to concentrate on the holiday movies playing on TV. They couldn't hold her attention. Nor could the mystery novel she tried to read after turning the television off. She paced restlessly through the house, knowing it would be a waste of time to try to go to bed. She wasn't even close to being sleepy.

You know where to find me. If you want to find me.

Lucas's words echoed so clearly in her head that

she could almost see him standing in front of her, saying them.

"No," she said aloud. "Don't do this, Rachel."

She couldn't help picturing him surrounded by his family this evening. How was he getting along with everyone? Was he mingling? Smiling? Laughing, maybe? Sharing family memories, swapping old stories?

It was hard to imagine Lucas in the middle of a crowd when she always thought of him as such a loner.

Had he thought of her tonight?

You know where to find me. If you want to find me.

She shook her head, as though she could physically dislodge the disturbing memory of his deep voice.

She couldn't sit here like this, moping over Lucas the way she had as a love-struck teenager. She had to do something to distract herself. So she concentrated, instead, on the improbable tale he'd told her during lunch.

She could hardly believe her brother had concocted such a wild story. Rachel herself had tried during the years to come up with a plausible explanation for their father's abandonment, but murder had never been one of the scenarios she'd imagined.

Poor Roger. He'd always been so angry. So sullen. So unreliable. Twenty-one at the time of his death, he'd dropped out of college, had been fired from two different jobs because he'd refused to follow directions, and had lived on a diet of beer and bitterness. And he'd had an almost pathological dislike for the McBrides, blaming them for almost every perceived injustice in his life.

Rachel had tried a time or two to make him see reason. She'd pointed out that Nadine had been a McBride only by marriage, and that none of the others had anything to do with Al's betrayal. She'd reminded him that Emily, especially, had been as deeply hurt as Rachel and Roger had been, and deserved their sympathy, not their antagonism.

But Roger would never listen to Rachel. The only member of his family who'd had any influence over Roger had been their father's brother, Sam. Sam had made a halfhearted effort to be a mentor to his fatherless nephew, but Sam had been almost as irrational as Roger where the McBrides were concerned.

Rachel had heard whispers that there'd been a history of some sort between Sam and Nadine, that Nadine had been involved with Sam before dumping him unceremoniously to marry the much older widower, Josiah McBride, Jr. After her marriage, Nadine had taken up with Sam's older brother, Al Jennings, engaging in an illicit affair that had finally led to a clandestine elopement.

Rachel wondered if Sam had ever found out about Roger's ridiculous theory that Josiah had murdered Nadine and Al.

She hadn't talked to her uncle since that scene in the café Tuesday. He'd been unreasonably furious with Rachel for being polite to Lucas and Emily, and she'd been annoyed with him for embarrassing her so publicly. They'd parted very coolly in the parking lot outside the café, making no plans to meet again.

The Jennings family had truly fallen apart, Rachel couldn't help thinking, while the McBride clan seemed to be thriving. Roger would have hated that. Sam probably did, too.

On an impulse, Rachel climbed the stairs to her grandmother's attic. She had been trying to organize some of her grandmother's belongings during the past few days, separating items to be sold from those to be placed in storage for now. She'd found several boxes of Roger's possessions, though she hadn't gone through them. Now she found herself wondering about that "proof" Roger had supposedly found to verify his wild tale of jealousy and murder.

Distraught by her son's death, Jane Jennings had dumped all his belongings into large cardboard boxes without taking time to go through them. She'd sealed the cartons with heavy packing tape and hidden them in this attic, where they'd remained undisturbed for fifteen years. Rachel broke two nails trying to open the first box before finally going downstairs for a knife.

She rummaged through her brother's things with a heavy heart, wishing they'd had a better relationship. Emily had been separated from *her* brother for a long time, and still looked at him now as though the sun rose and set in him. Rachel had never felt that way about Roger.

She dug through clothing, shoes, toiletries, accessories. Jane had packed everything—half-empty containers of toothpaste and deodorant, a used, disposable razor, a can of athlete's-foot spray. Rachel sighed, shook her head and closed the box, having found nothing out of the ordinary.

A second carton held books. Paperback murder mysteries, mostly, along with a few worn science-fiction novels. Roger had been an avid reader; Rachel couldn't help wondering if he'd begun to lose his ability to distinguish fact from fiction.

The third box Rachel opened held the contents of the desk that had been in Roger's room. His wallet, personal papers, bankbooks, tax forms. A sealed manila envelope held his high-school diploma and a certificate declaring him an honor graduate. Roger had been intelligent enough; he'd just never lived up to his potential.

At the very bottom of the box was another sealed manila envelope. It held something solid. Bulky. Rachel opened it almost absently, telling herself she was wasting her time. What had she expected to find, anyway?

A mud-caked leather wallet fell into her hand.

She stared at it blankly for a moment, thinking that it must have been Roger's. He'd obviously ruined it at some point and had switched to another.

So why had he kept this one?

She opened the wallet slowly, her fingers trembling.

A photograph stared up at her from a yellowed, weathered driver's license.

The wallet had belonged to Albert R. Jennings.

Rachel's long-lost father.

8

LUCAS WAS AWAKENED Christmas morning by a high-pitched shout of delight.

"I got my bicycle! Hey, everybody, Santa brought my bicycle!"

Lucas yawned and shoved a hand through his hair, noting that it was just after six-thirty. Christmas started early when there was a kid in the house, he thought.

He pulled on a sweatshirt and a pair of jeans, sliding his feet into his shoes without bothering with socks. And then he headed for the living room to see what else Santa had left beneath the tree—as if he hadn't helped place the stuff there only hours before.

Clay was practically bouncing off the walls of the living room. "Uncle Lucas, Uncle Lucas! Look what I got!"

Lucas made a production of admiring the shiny ten-speed bicycle he and Wade had spent nearly two hours putting together the night before. It had seemed like a simple enough project—until they'd realized the instructions were written in Martian. Lucas knew computers and Wade knew police procedures, but neither of them was a wizard with a wrench.

Lucas nodded toward the pile of presents beneath the tree. "Looks like Santa left more than one gift."

Clay nodded eagerly. "Daddy said for me to wait until everyone was up before I opened them. Are you up now, Uncle Lucas?"

Bundled into a fuzzy bathrobe, Emily slipped a steaming mug of coffee into Lucas's hand.

Lucas nodded at her in gratitude before turning back to the excited boy. "I'm up now."

Clay promptly pounced on the stack of brightly wrapped presents. Wade and Emily snuggled together on the couch and watched, Emily snapping pictures every few minutes, Wade smiling indulgently. Lucas sat in a comfortable armchair, sipping his coffee and wondering how it would feel to play Santa for his own kid.

An unlikely prospect, to say the least.

After exclaiming in delight over his haul from Santa, Clay turned his attention to the gifts remaining under the tree. "What about these?"

"Read the tags," Wade said. "You can hand them out."

Clay distributed the packages hastily, eager to find out what was in each one, whether they were for him or the others.

Emily gasped when she opened the diamond earrings from her brother. "Lucas, they're beautiful! But this is too much."

He smiled and shook his head. "It's the first present I've given you in fifteen years. Enjoy."

She was already fastening them into her earlobes. The diamond engagement ring that had been her gift from Wade glittered on her left hand.

Wade seemed almost as pleased with the fishing

reel Lucas had selected for him. "This is great, Lucas. The nicest one I've ever had. Thanks."

Lucas nodded. "You've obviously made my little sister very happy. I'm glad she met you...even if you are a cop," he added wryly.

Emily swiped at her eyes. "You really are a very sweet man, Lucas."

He cleared his throat and took another sip of his coffee to avoid having to reply.

Clay opened his gift from Lucas. "Oh, wow. Cool. A Rebelcom. Thank you, Uncle Lucas."

"You're welcome. I hope you enjoy it."

Emily looked a bit puzzled as she studied the beeping black plastic box. "What did you say that is?"

"A Rebelcom," Clay repeated, showing her the illuminated screen. "It's a portable computer game system. Tommy Porter has one, and it has the coolest games in the world on it."

"All nonviolent and entertainingly educational," Lucas assured them.

"Designed and marketed by Rebel Software Corporation of Los Angeles, California," Wade murmured, reading from the box the game had come in.

Emily looked at Lucas with suddenly narrowed eyes. "Rebel Software? Is that...?"

He shrugged. "When I got to California, I hooked up with another guy who was interested in computer games. We were in the right place at the right time. We found a couple of backers, hired a few brainy computer geeks, and we've all done pretty well for ourselves."

"You haven't opened *your* presents, Uncle Lucas," Clay said.

Lucas had been deliberately postponing that. He never quite knew how to act when people gave him things.

"Open the one from Daddy and me first," Clay insisted.

Lucas nodded and opened a wrapped box to reveal a pair of black leather driving gloves. "These are really nice," he said, feeling awkward. "Thanks, Clay. You, too, Wade."

"I helped pick them out," Clay said importantly. "Daddy has some and he likes them a lot. Do you like yours a lot, Uncle Lucas?"

"I like them a lot," Lucas assured the boy with a smile.

"Now open the present Mom got you."

Lucas still hadn't quite adjusted to hearing the boy refer to Emily as "Mom." Judging from Emily's misty expression, she hadn't either—but she obviously liked hearing it.

Lucas peeled the wrapping paper away from Emily's gift to reveal an intricately designed mahogany box, the top an inlaid mosaic of assorted exotic woods. The beautifully worked box had obviously been crafted by a talented artisan. Lucas studied it closely. "This is great, Emily. Was it made locally?"

"Yes. Paul Cabot is a local woodworker whose boxes are becoming very popular at local craft shows and galleries."

"I can see why. The guy is good."

Lucas pressed a nearly invisible latch to open the

box. He went very still when he saw the items nestled into the velvet lining.

"You didn't take anything with you when you left fifteen years ago," Emily said quietly. "Those are some of the things I thought you might like to have."

The heavy gold pocket watch had belonged to Lucas's maternal grandfather. His mother, who'd died when Lucas was only five, had kept it for him. There was also a small silver frame holding an old photo of Lucas's mother. He didn't remember her very well, but this photo matched his hazy memory of her—pale, fragile-looking, visibly nervous and unhappy. Whether she'd been that way before she'd married Josiah McBride Jr., Lucas couldn't have said, but marriage to the stern, difficult man couldn't have been easy for a woman with depressive tendencies.

There were some who'd said she'd died of pneumonia because she simply hadn't wanted to live.

The final item in the box was a slender, aged, soft-leather-bound Bible. On the inside, inscribed in his mother's flowery handwriting, were her name, Josiah's name and the date of their wedding. Beneath that was Lucas's name and the date of his birth.

Lucas closed the Bible and held it for a moment in both hands before setting it back into the box, along with the pocket watch and the small framed photo. "Thank you, Emily," he said quietly.

"You're welcome. If there's anything you want that belonged to Dad…"

"No. These things are all I want."

She nodded, her eyes a bit damp.

Clay broke the sentimental moment by diving back into his gifts, wondering aloud what to play with first.

Emily stood, tightening the sash on her robe. "I'll start breakfast."

Lucas and Wade both started to rise. "Need any help?" Wade asked.

She shook her head and motioned for them to remain seated. "You guys stay in here with Clay. I have everything under control."

Clay climbed unselfconsciously into Lucas's lap, holding his Rebelcom. "Will you show me how to work it, Uncle Lucas?"

Lucas glanced at Wade, wondering if he minded sharing Clay's attention on this Christmas morning. But Wade was smiling, so Lucas settled the boy more comfortably on his knee. "Turn it on here. This button controls the left side of the screen, and this one…"

Clay nestled against Lucas's chest and listened intently to his soon-to-be-uncle's instructions.

The telephone rang just as they finished breakfast a little more than half an hour later. Emily smiled and stood. "I'll get it. I'm sure it's one of our cousins, wishing us Merry Christmas."

But a moment later, wearing a curious expression, Emily lowered the kitchen extension phone and motioned for Lucas. "It's for you. She, um, didn't identify herself."

Lucas knew who it was even before he heard her voice.

"Lucas? It's Rachel. I'm sorry to interrupt you so early on Christmas morning, but I need to talk to you."

He heard the strain in her voice and he knew immediately that something was very wrong. "What is it?"

"Can you meet me?"

"Yes," he said without hesitation. "When?"

"Give me half an hour."

He didn't have to ask where she wanted to meet. "I'll be there."

LUCAS WAS WAITING inside the rock house when Rachel walked in. He'd spread a thick cotton quilt over the dirty floor, so they could sit comfortably on the cold stone. He was pouring steaming coffee from an insulated container into a mug as she walked in.

He placed the mug into her hands and pressed her downward, urging her to sit cross-legged on the quilt. "Sit down and drink this. Take your time."

He was watching her as if he was afraid she would collapse at any moment. Either he'd heard something in her voice when she'd called, or she looked even worse than she'd thought after her nearly sleepless night.

Rachel took the coffee and sank to the quilt, feeling her knees weaken now that she was actually here with Lucas. The brew was hot and strong, and she sipped it slowly, letting the warmth spread through her.

Lucas sat in front of her, without looking away from her face. "Take all the time you need. There's no other place I have to be."

She tried to smile. "I'm really not going to collapse, Lucas."

"Something has upset you."

"Yes. But I'm fine. I just want to talk to you about it."

"What is it? Did someone say something to disturb you?"

For just a moment, he was the young Lucas she remembered, fire in his eyes, willing to fight to defend her.

She laid a hand on his knee and shook her head. "No one said anything. It's something I found last night in a box of my brother's belongings."

Lucas went still. "What did you find?"

She'd brought a macramé shoulder bag to free her hands so she could climb the gate. She opened it and pulled out the crumpled manila envelope. "This."

Lucas accepted the envelope from her. "What is it?"

"Open it."

She kept her gaze on his face as he tilted the envelope to retrieve the contents. His eyes narrowed when the filthy wallet fell into his hand. He opened it slowly.

"Where did you say you found this?" His voice was strained as he stared at Al Jennings's driver's license.

"It was with Roger's things—in a box with the stuff from his desk. Mother packed everything without looking through it, so I doubt that she saw this."

Lucas flipped carefully through the contents of the wallet—the license, credit cards, insurance cards, faded photographs of Roger and Rachel.

There were several bills stuffed into the money pocket—two hundreds, a twenty and a ten.

"It's covered in dirt," Rachel commented, though she knew Lucas had noticed that for himself.

"Yes."

"It looks as though it was…buried."

"Like Nadine's bracelet," Lucas agreed.

Rachel swallowed. "Do you suppose Roger found it in the same place as the bracelet?"

Lucas closed the wallet and slipped it back into the envelope. "I think that's a good guess."

"Lucas…"

"Don't let your imagination run away with you, Rachel."

"But why would my father have left town without his wallet? Without any money? Without his driver's license?"

"Did your father have a car?"

She nodded. "A little two-seater sports car. My grandmother said he was going through a midlife crisis—he colored the gray in his hair, bought a sports car and started running around with Nadine."

"The car disappeared when they did?"

"Yes. Everyone assumed they left in it."

"They probably did."

"But why would my father's wallet have been buried with your stepmother's bracelet? Why…?"

Lucas covered her hand with his. "Maybe he decided to change his name."

"Then why leave the money?"

"I don't know," he said with a sigh.

"You think something is strange about this, too, don't you?"

He didn't answer for a while, but sat holding her hand in his, the envelope on the quilt beside him. "There are some things that don't add up," he admitted finally.

"Roger told you he didn't believe our father and Nadine left town. He thought they were murdered and buried on your property."

"That was his theory."

"Did you…ever look? For possible grave sites, I mean."

"No. I told you, I thought Roger was crazy. And then he died, and I was suddenly defending myself against a possible murder charge, thanks to a bunch of meddlers who swore they'd heard me threaten to kill Roger."

"*Did* you ever threaten to kill him?" Rachel asked softly.

Lucas's mouth twisted. "Probably. Roger and I were always mouthing off at each other, saying stupid things. But, Rachel, if I said it, I never meant it."

"I know you didn't kill him. You had an alibi."

"Actually…I didn't."

Her hand jerked in his. Lucas tightened his fingers to hold her.

She stared at him. "What are you talking about? Of course you had an alibi."

"You mean Lizzie Carpenter."

She nodded grimly. "Yes."

"I didn't sleep with her."

Rachel scowled. "Lucas, you spent the entire night with her. She told everyone so."

"She lied."

Rachel tugged at her hand. "Let go of me."

"No. Sit still."

"Lizzie told everyone you and she spent the night together. She showed me the charm you gave her."

Now it was Lucas's turn to scowl in confusion. "What charm?"

"A gold heart—exactly like the one you gave me," Rachel whispered, looking away.

After a moment of silence, Lucas cleared his throat. "Okay, let's start over. What the *hell* are you talking about?"

Still avoiding looking at him, her hand lying limply in his, Rachel answered. "As you know, Roger's body was held by the coroner for almost a week after he was found dead, while they investigated whether he'd died of accidental causes or…or something else. It wasn't until two days afterward that we could hold the funeral. My mother was in terrible shape. The rumors were already starting to fly that you'd had something to do with my brother's death. Sam was loudly demanding an investigation, and my mother said she'd always known the McBrides would destroy what was left of our family. I couldn't tell anyone I'd been seeing you, because I knew they would get hysterical and forbid me to ever have anything to do with you again."

"That was why I didn't call you during those early days. I knew your family needed you and that you couldn't be with me."

She stared at her hand in his. "Did you leave a bouquet of red roses at our door on the day of

Roger's funeral? They were addressed to me and they had no signature. My family assumed they were from my classmates. I thought maybe they were from you."

"They were."

She nodded as he confirmed her suspicions. "They were beautiful. They helped me get through that day, because I knew you were thinking of me, even though we couldn't be together. I thought that once everything had settled down, after Chief Packer had proven to everyone's satisfaction that you'd had nothing to do with Roger's death, you and I could start seeing each other openly at last. I knew Mother wouldn't like it…and I knew Sam would hate it, but I didn't care about him. I just wanted to be with you."

"But things didn't settle down," Lucas said grimly. "Packer was convinced I'd pushed Roger off that bluff. He was trying everything he could to prove it, even though he had no evidence. Sam was running around calling me a murderer, and most of the townspeople believed him, since they'd always suspected I'd come to no good, anyway. Packer hauled me in several times to question me. And every time, I told him I had no alibi for the night Roger died."

"Every time you said that, you only increased his suspicions about you. And then Lizzie Carpenter told everyone where you *really* were that night."

Rachel had to force her voice through her tight throat as she remembered the devastation she'd felt over Lizzie's revelation.

"Rachel…"

She swallowed and pressed on. "Lizzie and her mother came to our house the week after the funeral—almost two weeks after Roger died. While my mother cried all over hers, Lizzie and I went into the kitchen to make coffee. Lizzie told me what everyone was saying about you, and then she assured me that she knew you hadn't had anything to do with Roger's death. She knew, she said, because you had spent that entire night with her. That was the first time I had heard about it, though she'd already told Chief Packer and several others."

Rachel had had to listen to Lizzie rave about her "night of passion" with Lucas for nearly half an hour, she'd had to pretend that Lucas meant nothing to her, and that she didn't care who he'd slept with. It had been the most difficult half hour of her young life.

"And then she showed me the charm," she whispered, closing her eyes against the painful memories. "Like the one you'd given me. She said you'd given it to her that night—the night you spent with her."

Lucas's hand tightened around hers. His voice was low, urgent. "Rachel, she lied. I didn't give her a charm. And I didn't spend the night with her. I didn't even see Lizzie the night Roger died."

Frowning deeply, Rachel turned her head to look at him, studying his face intently. "You're saying you really had no alibi that night?"

"No. I drove to Atlanta—alone—and I spent the evening in a bar, drinking with a fake ID. I didn't get home until well after midnight. I wanted to think about the stuff Roger had told me, and to decide how much of it I should tell you. And I kept wondering whether he really would be able to break us up."

Rachel's mind was spinning. "But why did Lizzie say what she did? Did you ask her to lie for you, so you would have an alibi?"

"Of course not. That was all her idea." He drew a quick, sharp breath, then let it out in a sound of disgust. "Lizzie and I dated for a while in high school. But I never went out with her after I started seeing you. She kept trying to get me back—I don't know why. Called me all the time, followed me around. She annoyed the hell out of me, to be honest."

"Did you give her the charm while you were dating?"

"I *never* gave her a charm. You were the only one..." He stopped abruptly. "Hell."

"What?"

"Lizzie came into the jewelry store when I was buying that charm for you. She asked if I was buying it for Emily. I said no, but I wouldn't tell her who it was for. She was still in the store when I left."

"You think she bought the same charm for herself?" Rachel wasn't sure she believed all this, but she had never known Lucas to make up elaborate stories.

"Hell, I don't know. But it sounds like something she'd do."

"I still don't understand why she told everyone you'd spent the night with her. What did she hope to gain, if it wasn't true?"

"She thought she was doing me a favor. She

came to me one afternoon and she said she'd already been to Packer. She'd heard that I told Packer I didn't have an alibi, and so she'd provided me with one. She told him I'd lied to him to protect her reputation."

"She thought you'd be so grateful to her that you'd date her again?"

"That's exactly what she thought. I told her it wasn't going to happen. I said I didn't need her alibi, because I didn't kill Roger. She refused to change her story. She said she would look like a fool if she did, and she begged me not to dispute it."

"So you didn't."

"I didn't know what to do," he admitted. "I didn't want Lizzie lying for me, but I couldn't make her stop. When I tried to explain where I really was, no one believed me. Some people thought I'd spent the night with Lizzie. The others maintained I'd killed your brother. I knew if anyone found out you and I had been seeing each other, there would be even more speculation that Roger and I had gotten into a fight, and that I'd pushed him off the bluff."

"So you kept quiet."

"I kept quiet," he agreed flatly. "I neither confirmed nor denied Lizzie's story. And I watched the townspeople pull even further away from my family, some of them even refusing to let their kids play with my little sister because they didn't want any association with me. I hung around your house, trying to catch you alone for a minute, but someone was always there. And you didn't come out of your house for weeks."

"I was taking care of my mother. She had a breakdown of some sort and she wouldn't let me or my grandmother out of her sight. People came to the house to bring us food and try to talk to us about the scandal—they kept speculating about you and Lizzie, wondering if she was telling the truth, or if you'd killed Roger and were using her to cover for you. I didn't want to believe either possibility, but I was so confused. So overwhelmed by everything that had happened…"

"You were deliberately avoiding me, weren't you?"

"I suppose I was," she whispered. "The things Lizzie said…she made it sound so real. And it hurt me so badly to think that you and she…"

She swallowed. "You must have felt so alone during those weeks," she mused, thinking for the first time how it must have been for Lucas. "Did you try to talk to your father? Tell him what had happened? Ask for his advice?"

"I tried. I told him what Roger had said to me before he died."

Rachel swallowed. "You told your father Roger thought he was a murderer?"

"Yes. I asked if he'd had any knowledge that Roger had been hanging around our land, looking for evidence. If he had seen Roger the night he died."

"What did he say?"

Lucas's expression hardened. "He told me to get out of his house."

"He threw you out? Just for asking questions?"

Lucas nodded. "He told me he didn't like my implications and that he wasn't answering any questions raised by a Jennings. When I tried to push for answers, he told me to leave."

"That was the night you left town?"

He nodded again. "I tried to call you first. I thought you, if no one else, would believe me. I thought you could meet me, help me decide what to do next. You hung up on me."

She remembered the call. She'd heard Lucas's voice, and she had panicked, terrified that she would burst into tears and reveal everything. "My mother was in the room. I didn't know what to say to you. She and my grandmother were still distraught with grief over Roger. I was upset about losing the brother I had never known well enough, and I was still reeling from what Lizzie had told me. I felt so betrayed."

"You really thought I'd slept with her? After all the things I'd said to you that Saturday afternoon? All the promises I'd made to you?"

The hint of hurt in Lucas's voice put Rachel on the defensive. "I didn't know what else to think. Lizzie was so adamant about what had happened, and everyone told me you weren't denying it. And, Lucas, she had shown me the charm."

"She must have somehow found out you were the girl I'd been seeing. She must have wanted to come between us. I just can't understand why you believed her."

Rachel was finally able to jerk her hand from Lucas's grasp. She jumped to her feet, staring down at him. "I was eighteen years old. I had lost my brother, and my family was falling apart. And Lizzie *told* me it had happened. She seemed so defiant about it. So smug…"

"I had asked you to marry me," Lucas reminded her without getting up, his voice low, his eyes shuttered.

"And I told you I wanted to wait until after I'd gotten a college degree before getting married," she replied. "You said you'd wait, but I knew you were getting impatient with my hesitation about making love with you."

"You wanted to wait until the timing was right. I *was* impatient, but I understood. I didn't turn to Lizzie—or to anyone else—because you weren't yet ready for a physical relationship."

"I thought you had," she whispered. "I knew there had been other girls before me. I thought you'd gotten tired of waiting for me."

"You were wrong. And if you'd talked to me the night I called, I would have told you so."

Rachel looked blindly at the rock wall. "I was too young," she repeated in a whisper. "I didn't know what to do. Who to believe."

"I didn't know Lizzie had talked to you," Lucas conceded. "I didn't know about the charm."

Rachel dashed impatiently at her damp cheek. "I should have talked to you. I thought there would be time—I thought maybe you could explain everything, somehow, once I was ready to hear it—but then you were gone."

"It seemed the best thing for everyone. For you. For Emily. And maybe for me, too. I couldn't stay in Honoria knowing I was suspected of murder, and wondering if you thought I was guilty as well."

She met his eyes squarely. "I thought a lot of angry things about you, Lucas, but I never once believed you'd killed my brother."

"You know now that I had no alibi."

"That doesn't matter. You didn't kill Roger. You wouldn't have."

Lucas sighed and pushed a hand through his hair. "Which brings us back to square one. Roger died on these bluffs and neither of us knows why."

"He found your stepmother's bracelet and my father's wallet, and we don't know what that means either."

"And now the bracelet has disappeared again, and we don't know if it's a coincidence or connected in some way to Roger's wild theory."

Rachel sighed. "It's all very confusing."

So much had changed during the past few days. So many things she'd believed had been turned upside down. So much had happened fifteen years ago that she hadn't known about.

Time had seemed to fall away with every revelation, making it feel almost like yesterday that all these things had taken place.

Unfortunately, all her old feelings for Lucas were being brought to the surface, as well.

He caught her wrist and pulled her gently back down to the quilt. "Do you want some more coffee?"

She shook her head, folding her legs to one side. "No. We need to talk more about what I found. We should try to decide what, if anything, we need to do about it. We should..."

"First, there's something I want to give you." Lucas reached beneath the bench on the wall and brought out a small, wrapped package.

Rachel stared at it. "You brought something for *me?*"

"It's Christmas," he reminded her with a very faint smile.

She had been so lost in the past, so disturbed by the discovery of her father's wallet that she had almost forgotten what day it was. She certainly hadn't expected Lucas to give her a Christmas present.

"Open it."

Her fingers were unsteady as she removed the white ribbons and peeled away the red foil paper. A moment later, her eyes flooded with tears, blurring her vision of the leather-bound first-edition book of poetry Lucas had given her.

The memories had been hard enough to hold at bay before. Now, here in the rock house with Lucas at her side and a book of love poems in her hands, Rachel couldn't stop them from filling her mind.

Hungry kisses. Whispered promises. Shared secrets. Youthful dreams. Love so pure and so strong it had felt almost tangible, and had seemed destined to last a lifetime.

She didn't realize there was a tear on her cheek until she felt Lucas's thumb wiping it away.

"I didn't mean to make you cry," he murmured. "I thought you might like it."

"I do like it," she whispered, gripping the slender volume more tightly.

"Rachel…"

"I have a life, Lucas. I received a college degree, established a successful career, made a home for myself in Atlanta. I have friends. Goals. I almost got married once."

"Almost?" he murmured, his lips moving against her temple, his breath warm on her skin.

She shivered, and she couldn't blame the reaction on the cool December morning air. "I changed my mind. But my point is, I moved on. I left Honoria—and you—in the past. I'm not the same person I was fifteen years ago."

"Neither am I."

"No." But she was still fascinated by him. Still drawn to him in a way she couldn't explain and could certainly not deny.

He kissed her cheek. Her jaw. Turned her face toward him and brushed his lips over hers.

She was tired. Confused. Emotionally battered. She told herself she shouldn't be carried away under those circumstances, that this was a time for caution. Distance.

Lucas removed all remaining distance between them by pulling her into his arms and covering her mouth with his.

Rachel's arms went around his neck, all rational thought escaping her.

So much for caution.

9

It was chilly in the shelter. Even through the cotton quilt, the stone floor was cold and hard and bumpy beneath their knees. Rachel's jacket bunched around her, and she still held the book of poetry in her right hand, which dangled behind Lucas's head.

She was aware of those trivialities, just as she noticed the smoothness of Lucas's leather jacket, the faintly citrusy scent of his aftershave, the ragged edge to his breathing. She stored all the details in her mind, knowing she would replay them endlessly later.

His hands swept her body, plucking impatiently at her heavy clothes, finding pulse points that raced beneath his touch.

He released her mouth and buried his face in her throat, holding her so tightly she could hardly breathe.

"Rachel." Her name was a groan. Deep. Hungry. Almost angry.

Perhaps he resented as much as she did that they could still feel this way about each other. Still want each other so badly even though they knew how much pain they could cause each other.

She had hurt him. She knew that now. If everything he'd told her was true—and she had no rea-

son to believe it was not—he'd been alone and be-
wildered, suspected of something he hadn't done,
trapped by a jealous woman's lies and a small
town's gossip. Turned away by his own father.
And when he'd called Rachel, who had promised
to love him forever, she had hung up on him.

No wonder he'd felt he had no choice but to
leave town.

"I'm sorry," she whispered, her voice thick with
tears. "I should have given you a chance to tell me
what happened."

"No." He lifted his head, his hands gripping her
shoulders. "Don't start blaming yourself now. As
you said, you were young. And everything around
you was falling apart. To be honest, I'm relieved
that you didn't think me a murderer as well as a
philanderer."

"But if I'd known…"

"What would you have done? Would you have
told your mother you were in love with the guy she
believed had killed her son?"

"I…"

"If Packer had found out that Lizzie lied about
my alibi, if he'd known that you and I had been
seeing each other secretly and that Roger had
found out about it, if he'd learned that I told Roger
I would kill him before I let him take you away
from me, I would probably be in prison today."

"If I had talked to you that night when you
called, maybe you wouldn't have left town," she
murmured.

He lifted one shoulder in a slight shrug. "Maybe
that was for the best, too. With me gone, Emily had
a chance to make a place for herself here. You went

to college and got established in your career. And I started my own business in California which will allow me to live comfortably for the rest of my life."

She bit her lip and looked away. "You're saying that the past is better left alone. That everything is different now."

"No, that's not what I'm saying," he muttered, dragging her so close there could be no doubt he wanted her now as badly as he ever had. "Some things haven't changed at all."

He crushed her mouth beneath his, his hands biting into her hips, holding her against him.

Again, she was struck by the difference in the way he kissed her now. No tentativeness. No holding back. There was no need, now, to make allowances for youth, or inexperience, or girlish hesitation.

Rachel responded with a woman's passion. A woman's hunger. A woman's need.

Lucas kissed her until she melted against him. Until she clutched at him and greedily demanded more.

He stripped her coat off her shoulders and down her arms, tossing it carelessly aside. She didn't feel the cold through her sweater; in fact, she felt flushed with heat.

She tugged at his leather jacket, figuring he didn't need the extra warmth, either.

Lucas lowered himself to the quilt, tugging her down with him so that she was stretched over him. "No one has ever looked more beautiful to me than you," he murmured, brushing a strand of hair away from her face. "No one else has ever made me feel the way you do."

She ran her hands over his face, seeking and finding the differences fifteen years had made in him. The line of his jaw was harder now, more sharply defined. The shallow lines around his eyes and mouth only added to the attractiveness of his face, as far as Rachel was concerned.

"You were always the best-looking guy in Honoria," she told him. "You still are."

He cupped a hand behind her head and brought her mouth down to his. This kiss held a new tenderness, a sweetness that brought a lump to her throat. This was the Lucas Rachel had fallen in love with so long ago, the Lucas she had never stopped loving.

He nibbled her lower lip as she gave them both a chance to breathe. His hands slipped beneath the hem of her sweater, his palms cool and rough against her skin. She shivered in pleasure. Lucas draped her more snugly over him. Their blue-jeaned legs tangled.

She tried to maintain some semblance of rationality. "Lucas, what about the wallet? Shouldn't we...?"

"There's nothing we can do about the wallet now," he replied, speaking against her lips. "We'll look into it—later."

His right hand slid down her spine to her bottom, pressing her more snugly against the hard ridge beneath his jeans. A moan escaped her before she could swallow it.

"Lucas." His mouth was so temptingly close,

she couldn't resist kissing him. "We shouldn't do this."

"What's stopping us?"

For some reason, she couldn't think of one good answer. They were here—alone. Neither of them had anywhere else to be at the moment. They were unattached adults, and at least one of them had dreamed about this for years.

And it was Christmas—which had absolutely nothing to do with anything, except that Rachel was suddenly tempted to give herself a gift she'd been wanting for years.

Somehow Lucas's right hand had slipped between them, closing gently around her left breast. Rachel's breath caught as shattering sensations coursed through her.

So maybe she would be rational and practical later.

She pressed her mouth to his again.

Lucas pushed the lace cup of her bra out of the way, giving him better access to her sensitized nipple. She arched restlessly, her right knee bending, sliding up his leg.

"You used to slap my hand when I did this," Lucas said, circling his thumb in a way that made her gasp.

"Now I'll slap it if you stop," she murmured, emphasizing her words with a little wriggle.

His husky chuckle was a sweet reward. Lucas's laughter was so rare these days.

He lifted her higher against him, bringing her breasts level with his mouth. Rachel buried her hands in his hair and closed her eyes, allowing herself to drift on waves of sensation as he nuzzled beneath her sweater, his mouth unexpectedly hot against her tender flesh.

She didn't want to think about the past—or the future. She didn't want to think about buried bracelets or wallets, or long-standing family feuds. She wanted to live in this glorious moment, to fulfill a dream that had been with her almost longer than she could remember.

He loosened her jeans and slid his hands inside the back waistband, cupping her bottom. Rachel fumbled with the buttons on Lucas's shirt, wanting the same freedom to touch and explore that she was giving him.

His chest was hard. Solid. Lightly dusted with dark, soft hair that curled around her fingers when she ran her hands across it.

She slid downward on his body, pausing to kiss his jaw, his throat, his chest, his stomach. His breath was coming faster now. Rougher. She unsnapped his jeans and his stomach contracted forcefully.

Lucas was on the verge of losing some of the rigid emotional control he'd developed during the past fifteen years. It gave her a gratifying sense of power to be the one who'd brought him to this point.

He rolled suddenly, pinning her beneath him on the hard stone floor. She didn't care about the minor discomfort. Her heart pounded, her breasts ached, and there was a moist, throbbing emptiness between her legs. Lucas loomed over her, his hair tumbling onto his forehead, his dark blue eyes glittering with an almost feral hunger.

"I've dreamed of having you, here, like this," he

muttered. "I've wanted you since the first time I saw you sitting in the soda shop so long ago. I've never stopped wanting you."

She reached up with both hands to pull his mouth down to hers. "I want you, too," she whispered. "Make love with me, Lucas."

They were words she had wanted so badly to say before, but had never found the courage until now.

A look of regret crossed his face. "I wasn't prepared for this. I didn't expect to do more than talk with you this morning. I can't protect you, Rachel."

"I protect myself. I'm on the pill."

He cupped her face between his hands, looking at her steadily. "Do you want to see my health card?"

"Is there any reason I should?"

"No. Hell, I've practically been a monk for the past few years. All I seem to do is work and take meetings."

His wry tone made her smile. "That sounds familiar. I can hardly remember my last date."

Lucas kissed her deeply. Thoroughly. "I hear it's like riding a bike. Once you've gotten the hang of it…"

She smothered the rest of his joking comment by covering his mouth with hers.

Lucas's teasing mood changed as quickly as it had appeared. He was suddenly entirely serious.

In deference to the cool morning air, they removed only the necessary items of clothing. But Lucas still seemed to touch and claim every inch of her.

Because of the hard floor, Lucas rolled again to

his back, pulling Rachel on top of him to spare her his weight. She wouldn't have complained, regardless.

He guided her to him, murmuring words of encouragement and appreciation. All she could say was his name as he thrust deeply, powerfully into her.

For the first time since Lucas had left Honoria, Rachel felt complete.

His fingers bit into her hips. His head arched back, revealing his throat to her lips, and the edge of her teeth. He groaned and then gasped, and she knew he was thinking of nothing and no one but her.

For now—for this one perfect, precious moment—Lucas McBride was hers.

BUNDLED INTO their jackets, Lucas and Rachel sat side by side on the quilt, sharing the last cup of coffee. They hadn't said much since their muffled cries of satisfaction had died away. But neither was in a hurry to leave.

Lucas's arm rested behind Rachel's back, keeping her close to his side. She laid her head on his shoulder. "What time is it?"

"I don't care."

"Lucas…"

He sighed and glanced at his watch. "Almost noon."

"Is Emily expecting you for lunch?"

"I told her not to wait for me. What about your grandmother?"

"She's dining with her pastor and his wife. I was invited to join them, but I begged off several days ago. I wasn't in the mood to spend this Christmas with strangers. My grandmother thinks I'm spending time with old friends today."

Lucas kissed her temple. "We could stay here all day."

She smiled. "Did you bring food?"

"No."

"You'll get hungry."

He brushed his lips over hers. "I'll get by."

She nestled her head on his shoulder again. The euphoria of their lovemaking was beginning to fade a bit, allowing other thoughts to crowd in. Questions about the wallet she'd found among Roger's possessions. Concerns about the recent attack on Emily and whether it could in any way have been connected to the bracelet she'd worn. Worries about when Lucas would leave again— and whether he would say goodbye this time.

"Don't start worrying," Lucas murmured, seeming to read her mind. "Whatever happened in the past, there's nothing we can do about it now."

"When I saw that wallet last night, I couldn't help thinking about what Roger said to you. Lucas...what if he was right? What if my father and your stepmother really were killed?"

"By my father?"

"Who else? Roger found the things on McBride land. And your father became so angry when you asked about it that he threw you out of his house."

"You have to understand, Rachel, that I'm not defending my father out of loyalty and certainly not from affection. I'm not necessarily saying he was morally above murder. I just don't see him being that passionate, or that reckless. His coldness and his lack of any real emotion toward *anyone* were his worst flaws. I just can't see him caring enough about Nadine to have killed her to keep from losing her. More likely, he would have told her the same thing he told me—get out, and stay out."

"And that's what you told Roger?"

"Yes. And I believed it. I wouldn't have left Emily with our father if I believed he was a murderer."

"But you hadn't seen the wallet then."

"No," he admitted after a moment. "The bracelet was easier to dismiss than the wallet."

"Isn't it just possible that Roger's theory was right?"

"I suppose it's possible. Though very unlikely."

She tugged at her lower lip, her mind filled with possible scenarios. "What if Nadine killed my father and left town in his car? She could have lost the bracelet in the process."

"Again, highly unlikely. Nadine was five-three, maybe a hundred and ten pounds. Your father was six foot, easily two hundred pounds."

"A gun is a very effective equalizer."

He nodded. "But could she have managed to bury him? If this happened the way you suggested, she had to hide the body so well it hasn't been found in twenty-four years. And besides, I can't see Nadine leaving town without a penny to her name. She married my father because she thought he could provide for her. He made a decent salary and she wanted someone to support her so she wouldn't have to work. The rumors I've heard around town suggested that Nadine chose her lovers after her marriage based on how generous they were to her. Cash. Gifts."

"Gifts like heavy gold bracelets?"

"Probably."

"Do you think my father gave it to her?"

"I know *my* father didn't. He didn't do things like that. She'd had the bracelet a long time. As far back as I remember, actually. It was very recognizable, something many people would probably remember in connection to her."

"You said Emily found the bracelet after you left. She was wearing it when she was attacked in her house. Did she know it was her mother's?"

"I assume she did. The newspaper article identified it as an antique bracelet that had belonged to her mother. The writer must have gotten that from Emily, or from the police report."

Rachel lifted her head to look at him. "You haven't asked her about it?"

"No."

"Why not?"

"I didn't know how to bring it up," he admitted. "I didn't want to ruin her Christmas or her upcoming wedding by telling her the things Roger implied about our father. And she seemed so pleased that I'd come back, I didn't want her to think it was only to find out what had become of the bracelet."

"You came back because the bracelet was connected in your mind to possible violence, and you wanted to make sure your sister wasn't affected by it."

"Something like that."

"Or maybe you just needed an excuse to come home."

He cleared his throat. "I wasn't looking for excuses. I could have come home any time I wanted. I just thought it was better, for Emily's sake, if I didn't. And I was right. I got her to admit that people have been driving her crazy with questions since they've heard I'm back. Asking her stupid questions—like, is it true I've been in prison for the past fifteen years? Or am I really a Mafia hit man?"

Rachel stared at him in disbelief. "You're kidding."

"I wish. That old biddy, Martha Godwin, even stormed Wade's office, demanding to know why he would allow his son to be around a man who raised all kinds of hell around here before getting away with murder."

She winced. "Martha flagged me down when I went to the pharmacy for my grandmother yesterday," she admitted. "She asked if it bothered me knowing you were in town. I told her that you had every bit as much right to be here as I did, and that I should think people would have better things to do than gossip, especially at Christmas. She didn't say much to me after that, thank goodness."

"What about you?" he asked, turning the question back to her. "Did you volunteer to help your grandmother settle her affairs so *you* would have an excuse to come back?"

"I didn't know you were going to be here."

"Would you have come back if you'd known?"

Would she have come if she'd known she would see Lucas? If she'd had any clue they would end up here in the rock house again? If she'd known they would finally make love, even though it was without promises or commitments or words of love?

"Yes," she answered simply.

Whatever happened from this point, she would allow herself no regrets about this morning.

Lucas tightened his arm around her, as if her answer pleased him.

"What are we going to do now?" she asked him.

"This minute?"

Suspecting he'd deliberately misinterpreted her, she shook her head. "Are we going to forget about finding my father's wallet? Write it off as a mystery that will never be solved?"

Lucas was quiet for a moment. "I don't know what else to do about it."

"You don't think we should look around? To see if we can find any other clues?"

"Rachel, it's been fifteen years since Roger found the bracelet and, presumably, the wallet. Twenty-four years since Nadine and Al disappeared. Even if there's anything to find, we're talking about fifty acres of wooded land. It would take weeks, at a minimum, to search it all."

They didn't have weeks. Rachel bit her lip, remembering Lucas's plans to only stay through Christmas. He'd given no indication that he'd changed his mind.

"Maybe it's best to leave the past buried, so to speak," he went on. "As far as I can tell, the break-in at Emily's house was completely unrelated to any of this. She's safe and happy. You and your mother have dealt with the past in your own ways. I've got a life in California. What good would it do any of us to start poking around in old scandals?"

"Maybe we would find some answers to what really happened."

"Would it make you feel any better to learn that your father was murdered? Or that he and Nadine buried all evidence of their identities and took off to start a new life together? Or that one of them killed the other, then disappeared? Or maybe that your mother found them together and killed them? Or any of the other half dozen or more scenarios we could come up with if we let our imaginations get out of control?"

Rachel shivered, suddenly cold. "No. I don't suppose any of those possibilities would make me feel any better."

He pulled her closer. "I didn't think so."

"So you're saying we should forget it, then. Forget everything."

He rested his cheek against her tousled hair. "Not everything."

And what was *that* supposed to mean?

Rachel shook her head, drawing slightly away from him. "I'm not sure I can dismiss what I've found so easily. You've had fifteen years to think about what Roger said and to decide it meant nothing. This is all new to me. I need to look into it a bit more."

"And just how do you expect to do that? Are you planning on trekking through the woods with a magnifying glass? Nearly everyone who was closely involved with Al and Nadine is dead now."

"Everyone except my mother. And my uncle Sam."

The mention of her uncle made Lucas frown. But he ignored the name and asked, instead, "You don't think your mother knows something she hasn't told you?"

Rachel couldn't suppress a grimace at the thought of asking her mother anything about Al's disappearance. No answer could possibly be worth the melodramatic hysteria that question would surely trigger.

"No. Mother doesn't know anything more than we do—not as much, I'm sure. I'll go through the remainder of Roger's things. Maybe I'll find something else. And I haven't looked through my father's stuff yet. Mother did the same thing with his stuff as she did with Roger's—she crammed everything into boxes and demanded that they be taken out of her sight. Maybe my father had something that would give me a clue as to what he was planning."

Lucas shook his head. "I think you're wasting your time, Rachel. If there'd been anything more, Roger would have found it and produced it."

She shrugged. "It's my time to waste, isn't it?"

"Yes. I guess it is," Lucas said in that cool, neutral voice she'd found so annoying before.

She pushed herself to her feet, pulling her jacket more snugly around her. "You should probably go back to your family. Emily will want you to be there."

Lucas rose more slowly. "Rachel, what's wrong?"

She tried to smile. "Nothing. I just hate to keep you from your family at Christmas."

"Come with me to Emily's. There's plenty of food for one more."

Her smile suddenly felt a bit more natural. "Wouldn't *that* give the town something to talk about? A Jennings at a McBride family holiday table."

Lucas muttered an inelegant suggestion of what the town could do with its gossip. "Will you come with me?"

"Thank you, but no. I think I'll go look through Roger's things while my grandmother is out of the house for a while."

"You're wasting your time." he said again.

"Yes."

In more ways than one, probably, she almost added.

She picked up the manila envelope and the book Lucas had given her. "Thank you for the book of poetry. I'll treasure it always."

"I'll walk you to your car."

"No." She held up a hand to stop him. "This is a walk I'm getting used to making on my own."

He scowled, obviously not understanding what she meant. She couldn't fault him for that; she hardly understood her own behavior at the moment.

Rachel stepped in front of him and rose on tiptoes to press a kiss against his unsmiling mouth. "Do me one favor, will you, Lucas?"

"What?"

"Don't leave this time without saying goodbye."

He was frowning after her when she turned and walked away.

10

"So, you want to tell me where you were all morning?"

Lucas pulled his attention away from the other side of the room, where Emily and Clay were engaged in a serious-looking board game, and lifted an eyebrow at Wade, who sat in a chair near Lucas. "No."

Wade stretched his long legs in front of him and regarded Lucas over a soda can. His expression showed he was definitely in "cop mode," Lucas found himself thinking.

"You got a call just after the crack of dawn that obviously concerned you. You filled a thermos with coffee and took off—walking, I noticed—telling us you didn't know when you would be back. You came back with a frown that stayed all through lunch, and you've hardly said three words all afternoon. Did you meet Rachel Jennings?"

Lucas glanced quickly toward Emily. She was concentrating entirely on Clay, oblivious to the conversation between her brother and her fiancé.

"Quit being a cop. You're off duty."

"All hell's going to break loose if her uncle finds out you're seeing her."

"If I *were* seeing her, she's a grown woman. She doesn't answer to her uncle…or to anyone."

Wade's mouth crooked into a wry smile. "Got a Hatfield and McCoy thing going?"

Lucas didn't answer. He didn't actually know *what* kind of thing he had going with Rachel. She'd acted oddly when she'd left the rock house. Did she regret meeting him there? Was she sorry about what had happened between them?

Wade was still watching Lucas closely. "You play your cards close to the chest, don't you? You still haven't told me why you really came back to Honoria, or what you were hoping to find in those old files of Chief Packer's. I still don't know what went on between you and Roger Jennings fifteen years ago, and what's going on between you and his sister now."

"Nothing that's of any concern to the local cops," Lucas answered coolly.

"Are you sure about that?"

Only an improbable tale of murder and concealment, Lucas thought. He nodded. "I'm sure."

The board game must have ended. Emily crossed the room and perched on the arm of Lucas's chair, leaving Clay to put away the playing pieces.

Lucas looped his arm around her waist. "Who won?"

Emily laughed. "Are you kidding? He stomped me. What are you two talking about so seriously over here?"

"Your fiancé was just grilling me about where I went this morning."

Emily frowned. "Wade, that's none of our business."

Wade looked ruefully at Lucas. "Very clever," he murmured.

"Where you went is your own business," Emily assured Lucas emphatically, though she couldn't quite hide the curiosity in her eyes. "We won't pry."

"Speak for yourself," Wade said. "I get paid for prying."

"Not into my brother's business."

Wade looked at Lucas. "That remains to be seen," he murmured.

Emily looked warningly at Wade again, then patted Lucas's shoulder. "Is there anything I can get for you? Something else to eat or drink?"

"No, I'm fine. Thanks."

"Want to watch me ride my bike, Uncle Lucas?" Clay asked, appearing to hang hopefully on Lucas's knee.

"Sure, kid."

Wade glumly studied the attention Lucas was receiving. "A lesser man might be jealous at this point."

"You can come, too, Daddy," Clay assured him.

"Thanks, pal. I'll do that. Go get your jacket and your helmet."

Emily lingered behind with Lucas when Wade and Clay went outside. "It has meant so much to me to have you here today, Lucas."

"I've enjoyed the visit," he assured her.

"Won't you reconsider staying for the wedding? It just wouldn't seem complete without you there."

"Emily…"

"Just think about it, okay?"

He nodded, feeling like a heel—which didn't

seem quite right, since he was only doing what was best for Emily. Wasn't he? "I'll think about it."

He was rewarded by her quick, bright smile. "At least you didn't say no."

"Uncle Lucas! I'm ready. Come watch me."

Clay's eager shout drifted through the open front door.

Lucas chuckled and draped his arm around his sister's shoulders. "Sounds like we'd better get outside."

RACHEL FOUND NOTHING else of importance in her brother's things that afternoon. She went through everything in the attic, but there was nothing out of the ordinary. And she didn't find anything else that had belonged to her father.

She waited until her grandmother rose from a long nap after her lunch with the pastor.

"I've been sorting and packing this afternoon," Rachel said, trying to sound casual about it. "I can't find any of Dad's things. Do you know what Mother did with them?"

"Your uncle Sam offered to store them in that metal building behind his house," her grandmother replied. "You know how your mother was after your father left. She didn't want anything that belonged to him left around here. Sam said he would put the things away for you and...and Roger."

Rachel grimaced. She wanted to go through her father's things, but she didn't want to have to explain her reasons to her uncle. Sam was such a difficult man.

The doorbell rang, announcing the arrival of a

couple of ladies from her grandmother's church, making a Christmas call on their ailing friend. Rachel visited with them for a little while, serving eggnog all around. Then she excused herself, allowing the long-time friends to visit.

She spent the remainder of the afternoon reading poems from the book Lucas had given her, reliving the morning she'd spent with him—and wondering how she could get to her father's things without going through her uncle.

WADE AND EMILY went out Christmas evening to take Clay to a "living Nativity" at the First Baptist Church of Honoria. The church had provided the display every Christmas evening for the past thirty years and it had become a popular community tradition.

They asked Lucas to join them for the display and then dinner afterward, but he declined. "We don't really want everyone gawking at me instead of Mary and Joseph, do we?"

"Why would everyone gawk at you, Uncle Lucas?"

Lucas ruffled the puzzled child's hair. "Good question, kid. But it used to be one of the town's favorite sports."

"We'll be back early," Emily told him on her way out the door.

"Take your time. I can entertain myself."

He watched them drive away, then closed the door and walked into the living room. The multicolored Christmas-tree lights were reflected from every shiny surface in the room. Clay's toys lay tumbled on the carpet around the base of the tree, along with a few scattered scraps of colored paper that had been overlooked when Wade had walked through with a trash bag earlier.

There'd been laughter in the house that morning, Lucas mused. A child's squeals of joy. Christmas carols playing from Emily's stereo. The smells of coffee, bacon, made-from-scratch biscuits. Lucas imagined this had been the cheeriest Christmas this old house had seen in many years—maybe ever. He could envision many more happy Christmases to follow, especially when Wade and Emily had more children, as he was sure they would.

He wanted to be around to see those kids, he realized now. This is what he'd been afraid of—that once his sister was back in his life, he wouldn't want to let her go again.

And was he really going to be able to walk away from Rachel again—especially after this morning?

On an impulse, he picked up the phone and dialed a number he found in the telephone book. He was relieved when Rachel answered.

"I wanted to make sure you're okay."

"I'm fine, Lucas. I just sent my grandmother off to bed, and I was thinking about turning in early myself."

"Tired?"

"Yes. I didn't sleep very well last night, after finding...well, you know."

"Yes."

"Have you had a nice day with your family?"

"Not bad. I spent most of the afternoon watching Clay ride his new bike."

"You've become very fond of him, haven't you?"

"He's a cute kid."

"They're going to miss you when you leave."

"They'll be busy starting their new life as a family. The don't need me hanging around."

"Are you...leaving tomorrow?"

The faint break in her voice made him frown. Was it going to be as hard for Rachel to walk away as it was for him?

"I, er, don't know," he answered awkwardly. "There are a few more things I might check out here first."

"What things?"

"I thought I might talk to the O'Brien kid. The one who broke into all those houses last fall. Wade said the kid admitted to all the other incidents, but swears he had nothing to do with the attack on Emily. Wade doesn't believe him. I'd like to hear the kid's denials myself—just to satisfy my curiosity."

"Will you be allowed to talk to him?"

"I'll talk to him." Lucas had no doubt he could get to the kid, one way or another. "Did you go through the rest of your brother's stuff this afternoon?"

"Yes. I didn't find anything of particular interest. I didn't have a chance to go through my father's things, though. My grandmother said they're all stored at my uncle's house."

Lucas scowled—as he always did when Sam Jennings's name was mentioned. He'd always disliked the guy, and thought his unreasonable hostility toward the McBrides bordered on lunacy. The knowledge that Jennings had been causing trouble for Emily made Lucas want to find him and bash his teeth in.

But that wasn't the way he behaved these days, he reminded himself, practicing the hostility-control methods he'd developed since he'd left Honoria. "You aren't going to tell him what you're looking for, are you?"

"What would I tell him?" she asked reasonably. "*I* don't know what I'm looking for. But, no. I wasn't planning to say anything to Sam."

Lucas didn't like the idea of Rachel having anything to do with Sam Jennings, even if he was her uncle. "Maybe it would be best if you leave your father's stuff alone for now. After all, there's probably nothing to find. And your uncle is bound to wonder what's going on."

"I'll tell him I just want to look through the stuff for sentimental reasons. I have every right to my father's belongings."

"I know. I just can't stand your uncle. I don't trust him."

She laughed softly, ruefully. "Really, Lucas, you should learn to be more outspoken about what you're thinking. It can't be good to bottle up your feelings this way."

He chuckled reluctantly. "I guess that wasn't very tactful, was it?"

"Tact has never been a word I've associated with you."

"So you'll leave your father's things alone for now? At least until I've had a chance to look into this more?"

"I'll think about it."

He was aware that she was making no promises. He was equally aware that he had no right to demand any from her.

"I want to see you again, Rachel."

"When?"

Now, he wanted to answer. Instead, he said, "To-morrow. Have dinner with me."

Which, he realized, meant he'd just committed himself to another full day in Honoria.

"I would like to have dinner with you, Lucas."

He nodded in satisfaction. They had just made an official date. He supposed it was about time.

"My grandmother is usually in bed by eight o'clock. I can meet you somewhere afterward, if you don't mind waiting that late to eat."

"You forget, I've lived in California for most of the past fifteen years. Eight o'clock doesn't seem that late. And we don't need to meet anywhere. I'll pick you up."

"What if someone sees us?"

"Then they see us." He, for one, was tired of sneaking around.

"Fine. I'll see you at eight, then."

"Fine. Er...good night, Rachel."

"Good night, Lucas."

He hung up the phone, then leaned back in the chair with his hands behind his head, and gazed at the lights on the Christmas tree.

RACHEL KNEW Lucas wanted her to stay away from her uncle, and she had no real desire to spend time with Sam, anyway. But her discovery of that wallet nagged at her. It just didn't make sense that her father would have buried the wallet and its contents. Lucas was probably right that she would find no explanations among her father's things, but she had an almost overwhelming compulsion to see for herself.

After spending Saturday morning trying to talk herself out of doing so, she drove to her uncle's house late that afternoon, thinking she would only stop by for a few minutes, and if the opportunity arose, she would ask about her father's things. She was relatively sure she could bring it up in such a way that Sam wouldn't find her request unusual.

It had been years since Rachel had been to her uncle's house. As far as she could tell, he'd made few changes to the white-shuttered, redbrick farmhouse on the outskirts of town. Several outbuildings surrounded the house. There was a detached, three-car garage in addition to the two-car garage connected to the house. A workshop. Two metal storage buildings.

Her uncle, it appeared, was a pack rat.

He was also not home.

Rachel stood for some time on Sam's front porch, trying to decide what to do. She shouldn't even consider going into the storage buildings without her uncle's permission, of course. But she was only interested in her father's things—which her uncle had offered to save for her, after all.

The buildings were probably locked, she told herself, even as she walked toward the first one. Sure enough, there was a heavy padlock on the door. The second building was secured in the same manner.

"Darn."

She really should wait for Sam, she thought, even as she made her way to the detached garage. The big doors were locked. As was the smaller door on the side. Rachel peered through a dirty window. A couple of tarp-covered vehicles sat inside—as well as a stack of cardboard boxes against one wall.

She frowned, pushing her nose nearly against the side-hinged window. She gulped when it swung inward. Either Sam had forgotten to lock the window, or the old lock had just given way when Rachel leaned against it.

"No, Rachel," she said aloud. "You are not climbing through this window. You have no right."

But she couldn't stop looking at those boxes. They looked a lot like the ones she'd found in her grandmother's attic.

"You're too old to climb through windows."

But she had climbed the gate across the lane several times now. Easily. All she'd have to do now was step over a low sill.

She shouldn't. But would Sam really mind if she told him she was only looking for her father's things?

She'd had a week full of reckless, daring, impulsive actions. What was one more? She stepped over the sill.

Skirting the two covered vehicles in the three-car garage, she headed straight for the boxes. It was almost with a sense of inevitability that she saw her mother's handwriting on the outside. "Al's things."

Rachel sighed and rubbed a finger over the stark black letters. How must her mother have felt, packing up her husband's belongings, knowing that he had abandoned her and their children for another woman?

She winced as the questions brought back the sense of overwhelming betrayal *she* had felt when her father left her. And, later, when she had been told Lucas had spent the night with Lizzie Carpenter. She'd been devastated. She could only imagine how her mother must have felt.

Learning that Lizzie had lied to her about Lucas had shaken Rachel so much that she still didn't know quite how she felt about it. If she dwelled on it too long, she would become fixated on how much time she and Lucas had been apart—and how much might have been different if she had taken his call the night he left.

The sealing tape on the boxes was yellowed and brittle, but still securely adhered. Rachel plucked at it futilely for a few moments, then looked around for something sharp for cutting. She didn't immediately see anything useful. The garage was clean, with very little in it besides the shrouded vehicles and the neatly stacked boxes. There weren't even any shelves along the walls, though a door at the back of the garage probably led into a storage room.

She stood and started through the shadowy room toward the door. She stumbled when her foot caught in the corner of a dusty car cover.

She hastily made a grab for the tarp. A glimpse of bright orange made her go still. Very slowly, she lifted the cover and looked at the classic two-seater sports car beneath.

Want to go for a ride in my magic pumpkin, princess?

Staring at the car, she could almost hear her father's voice.

It couldn't be the same one, she told herself dazedly. She hadn't seen her father's car since she was nine years old. It was just a coincidence that her uncle also owned an orange two-seater.

Moving as if in an eerie dream, she circled the hood, trailing her fingers along the time-dulled paint.

Her father had kept his sunglasses in the car. When he'd slid those aviator-styled glasses on his nose, Rachel had thought he was the most handsome man in the world.

She reached inside the vehicle and opened the tiny glove box, reaching inside as nervously as if she thought a mousetrap might clamp down on her fingers. And then she pulled out the sunglasses.

So many questions were spinning inside her head. Had her father left the car with his brother? Had Sam known Al and Nadine were planning to run away together? Maybe he'd even helped them. Maybe he'd given Al money, so that burying a wallet full of cash hadn't been any big deal.

Maybe Sam had only pretended to be as shocked and outraged as everyone else when Al and Nadine disappeared.

Not certain what she was looking for now, Rachel reached into the glove compartment again. What she pulled out this time made her gasp.

The heavy, gold-link bracelet gleamed dully in her hand. It looked old. Solid. Expensive.

It looked very much like the one Lucas had described to her. The bracelet that had been taken from Emily's wrist.

The small door at the front of the garage rattled. It was the only warning Rachel had before her uncle stepped inside.

He looked at her. At the uncovered car. And at the bracelet in her hand. And then he sighed.

"I really wish you hadn't done this, Rachel."

11

It seemed that nearly everyone had plans for Saturday afternoon. A wedding shower was being given for Emily by her aunts and cousins. A large number of Emily's friends and co-workers were expected to attend.

Bobbie and Ernestine had declared that men had no place at a shower, so the male members of the family were bundled off to Emily's house to spend the afternoon watching football. Lucas waited until Caleb McBride and his sons were settled in front of the TV, along with Kit Pace and Savannah's teenage son, Michael. Clay played patiently with Trevor's toddler son. Seeing that everyone else was occupied, Lucas drew Wade out to the front porch.

"Feel like taking a walk in the woods with your future brother-in-law?"

Wade studied Lucas's face. "Why?"

Lucas rubbed the back of his neck and grimaced wryly. "What would you say if I told you we're looking for buried bodies?"

"I'd say that's not very funny."

"It wasn't meant to be."

Wade opened the door and spoke into the living room, raising his voice to be heard over the blaring television. "Lucas and I need to go out for a while. Can you guys keep an eye on Clay for me?"

Without looking away from the game, Trevor waved a hand. "We'll watch him. Take your time."

Wade zipped his jacket. "Okay. Let's walk in the woods."

A slender blond man in a World-War-II-style leather bomber jacket with a Sherpa collar stepped around the corner of the house. "You guys mind if I come along? I really don't like football."

Lucas frowned at Blake Fox. "You spend a lot of time eavesdropping on private conversations?"

Blake responded with a cocky grin. "You might say I'm somewhat of an expert at the art."

Lucas debated, then decided maybe a P.I.'s perspective would be useful. "Come on, then."

Blake fell into step with them. "What's this about buried bodies?"

As they walked the trail toward the rock house, Lucas told them the full story. That his mother had died young, leaving Josiah a widower with a young son to raise. That Josiah had decided, for some reason, to marry Nadine Peck, one of the "wild women" of Honoria. That Nadine had begun a clandestine affair with Al Jennings after the birth of her daughter—an affair that had come to light when Al and Nadine had run away together, leaving their spouses and children behind without a word of explanation.

"Want me to look into it?" Blake asked. "There's a good chance I can find out what became of them."

"Let me tell you the rest of it first."

Lucas went on to detail how, nine years after Al and Nadine's disappearance, Roger Jennings had come up with the theory that they had never left town at all. That they had, in fact, been murdered. And then Lucas described the dirt-encrusted gold bracelet Roger had thrown at him only a few days before he'd died in a fall from a thirty-foot bluff.

Wade reacted strongly to that bit of information. "The bracelet stolen from Emily had been dug up by Roger Jennings?"

Lucas nodded grimly. "I hid it, myself, before I left town, but Emily apparently found it and started wearing it."

"She gave me the impression she found it among her father's things after he died last spring."

Lucas shook his head. "That's not likely. I haven't talked to her about it, though."

"And from finding that bracelet, Roger concluded his father had been murdered?"

"He apparently found something else. Something I didn't know about, myself, until Rachel showed it to me yesterday." He told them about the wallet and its contents.

"Now *that's* interesting," Blake murmured. "Leaving the driver's license behind—maybe. But the cash? Unusual."

"That's what I thought." Lucas led them into the clearing at the end of the path. "This is where Al and Nadine apparently met for their trysts. Rachel and I used to spend a lot of time here, too."

"Rachel. Roger's younger sister?" Blake asked, following the story with a frown of concentration.

Lucas nodded. "Roger saw her here with me while he was looking for clues, or God knows what, and he went ballistic. He came to me the next day."

"He ordered you to stop seeing his sister?" Wade hazarded.

"He said he'd kill me if I didn't."

Wade's expression didn't change. "And what did you say to that?"

Lucas knew exactly what kind of risk he was taking when he looked the chief of police in the eyes and replied, "I told him I would kill him before I let him come between us."

Blake coughed, then scooped up three pinecones from the ground at his feet and began to juggle them.

Ignoring Blake, Wade continued to look narrowly at Lucas. "You told me you didn't push Roger Jennings off that bluff."

"I didn't. I wasn't here the night Roger died."

"You were with the Carpenter girl." Wade repeated the accepted fact with a rather skeptical expression.

"I wasn't here," Lucas repeated. "I had nothing to do with Roger's death. I can only assume it was an accident. He was either looking for evidence or hoping to catch me with Rachel, and he somehow stumbled off the path."

"Where *was* Rachel?"

Lucas scowled at Wade. "Don't start that again..."

"It's a legitimate question, Lucas. You said Roger was trying to break the two of you up. She could have been as determined as you were to prevent that. She wouldn't have known, of course, that you were seeing another girl at the same time. The one you spent the night with when her brother died."

"Rachel," Lucas said between his teeth, "was out of town that night. She'd gone to Atlanta with her mother and her grandmother to do some shopping. They returned to the news that Roger's body had been found at the bottom of the bluff by a couple of hikers."

Wade nodded. "Just wondering."

"The only reason I've told you all of this is because one detail still concerns me, and I thought you should be aware of it."

"The attack on Emily," Wade murmured.

Lucas nodded grimly. "It just seems odd that the bracelet disappeared violently again. When I heard about the other break-ins, I convinced myself that it was only coincidence. But I talked to Kevin O'Brien this morning."

"How the hell...?"

"I managed," Lucas interrupted. "He swore to me, just as he did to you, that he did not break in to Emily's house. And, Wade, I believe him."

Wade grimaced. "He had reason to deny it, of course. There was an attack involved in that break-in, unlike the others. Which makes the charges all the more serious."

"I know he had reason to lie. And I'm sure he's damned good at it. But I know the kind of punk he is. Hell, I *was* that kind of punk, except that I never got bored enough to break in to houses. He didn't take Emily's bracelet."

"And that worries you. You think she was targeted strictly because of the bracelet."

"Even if someone was specifically after the bracelet—for whatever reason—Emily should be safe now. I just think you should be aware of what

I've learned today. You should know that there's another thief around here somewhere. It wasn't Kevin O'Brien.''

Blake tossed the pinecones high above his head, juggling them skillfully. ''Looks to me like you still need to find Al and Nadine.''

Lucas turned to him. ''Why?''

''Because it's the only way you'll ever know for certain that Roger's theory wasn't true.''

''I still can't believe my father killed anyone.''

''Motive and probability.''

Becoming reluctantly mesmerized by the dancing pinecones and Blake's cryptic words, Lucas asked, ''What the hell are you talking about?''

Blake let the cones fall and stuffed his hands into the pockets of his jacket. ''Not long after Roger Jennings decided that someone whacked his father, Roger took a mysterious fatal dive, right?''

And Rachel had accused *Lucas* of having no tact! Lucas stared at Blake through narrowed eyes. ''Something like that.''

''Okay, we know you had a motive to kill Roger. So did Rachel.''

Lucas almost growled in frustration. ''We did *not*...''

Blake held up a hand. ''I didn't say you did it, I'm just saying you had a possible motive. Just as your father could have had reason to want to kill his cheating wife and her lover.''

''So who else would have a motive to kill Nadine and Al?'' Wade asked. ''Assuming they *were* killed, of course,'' he clarified hastily.

''Jane Jennings,'' Lucas muttered, reluctantly going along. ''Not that I believe she did.''

"Low probability. But a definite motive," Blake agreed. "Who else?"

"Nadine could have killed Al and split," Lucas said, remembering some of the improbable scenarios he had thrown at Rachel. "Again—not probable without help."

"Or Al could have killed Nadine," Wade suggested.

Lucas huffed impatiently. "Or no one was ever killed, at all—the likeliest probability. Al and Nadine ran off to play house somewhere and Roger walked off the path and into a free fall."

"No one has heard from Al or Nadine since they left town?" Blake asked.

Lucas shook his head. "Not as far as I know."

"Nadine had no family?"

"She was estranged from the few relatives she had, long before she disappeared. It's unlikely she's ever contacted any of them since."

"And Al?"

"Rachel told me no one's heard from him. He had no family left, either…except for his brother."

"Sam Jennings," Wade supplied. "He's a local dentist. Hates McBrides enough to accuse Emily of embezzlement a few months back. Turned out it was one of his own employees. But he really seemed to want it to be Emily."

Blake looked quickly at Lucas. "Why does he hate McBrides?"

Lucas shrugged. "The guy's crazy. Always has been."

"But *why?*" Blake insisted.

Lucas wondered if he could make Blake understand the old-fashioned, long-standing Southern feud. "My great-grandfather and Sam's grandfather hated each other. I never knew what started it, but they spent their entire lives fighting and competing. They raised their sons to carry on the tradition, so that Sam's father and my grandfather were lifelong enemies. So there's been a long history of animosity. It didn't help that Sam was briefly engaged to Nadine Peck before she dumped him to marry my father."

Blake lifted an eyebrow. "Sounds like a plot from a Southern soap opera."

Lucas didn't smile. "Tell me about it."

"So Nadine dumped Sam, married your father, then ran off with Sam's brother."

"Yeah."

"Sam must have really hated Nadine after that."

"I suppose. Even though Nadine was only a McBride by marriage, it all just added fuel to the feud in his bitter mind."

"Sam has never married?"

"Twice," Wade supplied. "Twice divorced. No kids."

"How do you think he reacted when he found out Nadine was having an affair with his brother?"

"From what I've heard, no one knew about Al and Nadine until they disappeared together," Lucas answered.

"And no one knew about you and Rachel," Blake reminded him. "But Roger found out, anyway."

Lucas rubbed the back of his neck, thinking about the implications of Blake's words. Sam's was the first name that actually made some sense to Lucas. He had a motive—if jealousy and bruised ego could be seen as grounds for murder—and was much more likely to have lost his temper and turned violent than the others on the short list.

He thought of his conversation with Rachel the night before. He hoped she'd paid attention when he'd suggested she stay away from her uncle. Or was Blake only making him paranoid?

"You don't know where, exactly, Roger found the bracelet and wallet?" Blake asked Lucas, glancing at the woods around them.

"No. But I think it was somewhere in this area, in the vicinity of the rock shelter."

Blake studied the landscape. "That way leads to the bluffs?"

"Yeah. It's a thirty-foot drop to the creek."

Blake nodded decisively. "You know the bluffs. You look in that area. I'll take the section north of the rock building. Wade, you look south."

Lucas lifted an eyebrow. "What are we looking for?"

"We'll know it if we find it," Blake replied with his own brand of logic.

"Blake, it's been twenty-four years. And Chief Packer scoured this area when Roger took his dive, looking for evidence against me."

"Then we're probably wasting our time. But it beats watching football. Or going to a wedding shower."

"I *like* football," Wade muttered, but he walked away obligingly, his eyes trained on the ground.

Lucas sighed and headed for the bluffs.

LUCAS WALKED up to Rachel's door just before 8:00 p.m. The back of his neck itched, making him feel as though dozens of eyes were watching him from behind curtains and window blinds. He hadn't felt that way since he'd left this town.

He squared his shoulders and held his head high, telling himself he didn't care if half of Honoria was watching him. He and Rachel had nothing to hide now.

Mindful that Rachel's grandmother could already be sleeping, and expecting Rachel to be waiting for him, Lucas tapped lightly on the front door.

Over dinner, he'd decided, he would tell her about the search he, Blake and Wade had conducted all afternoon. It had netted them a few beer cans, a rusted belt buckle that could have belonged to anyone, a broken flashlight and…Blake's discovery…a filthy lace bra. The undergarment hadn't been there twenty-four years. A few months, at the most—proving that the gate hadn't been as effective a deterrent against trespassers as whoever installed it had hoped.

They had found nothing that indicated a murder had ever taken place there. Lucas hadn't really expected to find anything, of course. He had let his imagination carry him away, just as Roger's had fifteen years ago.

Rachel would probably be amused by the whole story. Maybe.

So, where was she?

He tapped on the door again, a little louder this time.

The door flew suddenly open. "There you are. I've been…"

The frail-looking, elderly woman in the doorway stopped and stared at Lucas. "Who are you?"

Lucas cleared his throat. "I'm a—er—friend of Rachel's. I'm here to take her to dinner."

Jenny Holder's faded blue eyes suddenly narrowed. She held her glasses higher on her nose and peered at him. "You're the McBride boy!"

At thirty-five, it had been a while since Lucas had been called a boy. "Er...yes, ma'am. Lucas McBride."

"And you're here to take Rachel to dinner?"

"Yes. She's expecting me."

"She's not here."

Lucas frowned. "What do you mean? She told me to pick her up at eight."

"She's not here," the woman repeated flatly. "I don't know where she is."

Several wild thoughts flashed through Lucas's mind. The woman was lying, trying to keep him from Rachel. Or Rachel had left town without saying goodbye. Paying him back for doing the same to her—letting him know how it felt.

Wherever she had gone, he would find her.

He managed to get a grip on his imagination, which had been showing an uncharacteristic tendency to run away with him today. "You were expecting Rachel when you opened the door."

The woman nodded her notably unsteady head. "I can't imagine where she's gone. I expected her hours ago. She told me she was going out tonight, but she said she'd be here to help me into bed first."

"Are all her things still here?"

"Of course they are. She didn't leave town. She just left to run some errands."

"When was that?"

"Maybe four hours ago. She said she'd only be gone an hour or so."

Lucas's stomach had begun to clench. A chill slithered down his spine. "Mrs. Holder, do you know where Rachel went?"

"No. She just said something about some errands. Why was she going out to dinner with you, Mr. McBride? I didn't realize you and my granddaughter even knew each other."

"Yes, ma'am. We do."

She studied him a moment longer. "Some people around town say you killed my grandson."

"Those people are wrong."

"I think a lot of your sister. She's a nice girl. A real asset to this community."

"She's the best of the McBrides," Lucas said simply. "Mrs. Holder, I'm worried about Rachel. If you have any idea where she might be..."

"I wish I did. I'm worried, too."

"Will you be all right while I try to find her?"

She nodded. "I'll be fine. Go find Rachel."

"Lock your door," Lucas ordered. "And wait by the phone. I'll be checking in."

He waited only until she had closed the door before he turned and dashed toward his car. He grabbed his car phone and dialed Emily's number. Rachel would have called him, he told himself. Maybe she'd just been delayed somewhere...

"It's Lucas," he said when Emily answered, not even giving her a chance to speak. "Have you heard from Rachel?"

She seemed surprised by the question. "No. Was she supposed to call?"

His hopes sank. Something was wrong, damn it. And he needed help. "Is Wade there?"

"Yes, he…"

Too distracted to be polite, he interrupted her. "I need you to do something for me. Rachel's grandmother is alone in her house and she needs someone with her. You know her friends. Her pastor, maybe. Will you call someone?"

"Of course. What's…"

"I'll explain later. Can you put Wade on now?"

A growing sense of urgency was driving Lucas. He wanted to find Rachel, and he wanted to find her *now*.

He hardly gave Wade a chance to identify himself before launching into an explanation.

Wade listened, then asked, "Where do you think she could have gone?"

"The last time I talked to her, she was considering going out to her uncle's place—to look through her father's things that are stored there."

"Damn. But, Lucas, you can't go out to Sam Jennings's place. He's liable to shoot you on sight—whether he knows anything about Rachel or not."

"That's why I'm calling you. Will you meet me?"

"Where?"

Lucas named an intersection that was close to the turnoff to Sam's place. "I'll be waiting for you at the Exxon station there. Hurry."

"All right. And, Lucas—wait for me. I don't want you talking to Sam Jennings without me there. Remember, it's possible he has no idea where Rachel is."

"Just don't take too long to get there." Lucas ended the call and started his car.

HE REACHED the service station ahead of Wade, and sat drumming his fingers on the steering wheel, anxious to be on his way. He was giving Wade five minutes, he told himself, and then he was leaving without him.

He needed to find Rachel.

It wasn't only his imagination making him worry now. Rachel had told him to pick her up at eight. Even if she'd stood *him* up—and he didn't believe she would, no matter how he'd treated her in the past—she wouldn't have given her grandmother cause to worry. She wouldn't have been gone four hours without calling to check in.

Not if she was able to call.

That thought went straight to his gut. He couldn't wait any longer. He had to know if she was at her uncle's house. If she wasn't...well, he would deal with that fear when it was justified. He reached for the gearshift, then paused when a familiar dark Jeep turned into the service-station lot. The Jeep pulled up beside him, and the driver's window lowered, revealing Wade and Blake inside.

Lucas lowered his own window. "It's about time you got here."

"I came as fast as I could. Blake showed up just as I was leaving and wanted to come along. He said he had a feeling something was going on."

Lucas wasn't discounting anyone's "feelings" at the moment. He had a bad one of his own to deal with. "Let's go," he said.

Wade wasn't letting Lucas out of his sight. "Leave your car parked here. We'll take mine."

Lucas grumbled, but turned off the engine, pocketed the keys and locked the doors. He didn't like taking orders. But right now, his only concern was for Rachel.

Wade didn't have to ask where Sam's house was. He drove to it unerringly, pulling into the driveway and parking close to the front door. Lucas was out of the car almost before the engine died. Wade caught up with him, and insisted that Lucas let him go first.

No one answered when Wade rang the doorbell, Lucas and Blake hovering close behind him. There were a few lights burning inside, but the curtains were drawn. There was no way of knowing if anyone was inside.

Growing impatient, Lucas took a step backward. "I'm going to look around."

Blake turned. "I'll go with you."

"Now, wait a minute, you two. We don't have a warrant. We can't just start searching Jennings's property."

Lucas didn't slow down. "I'm not a cop."

"No, you're a trespasser. Lucas—"

Blake was right at Lucas's shoulder as Lucas headed for the back of the house. Lucas heard Wade mutter something unintelligible and then he fell into step behind them.

Two storage buildings were secured with heavy padlocks.

"I could break those if I had a crowbar," Lucas muttered.

"Don't even think about it," Wade warned him.

"Maybe we should call Rachel's house. See if she's checked in yet."

But Lucas was watching Blake, who was headed for the detached garage. A tiny penlight in his hand illuminated fresh tire tracks in the ground, which was still damp from the heavy rains of the past week.

Lucas frowned and followed the P.I.

The tire tracks indicated that a car had very recently been driven into the garage. The doors were locked. Lucas looked at Blake, who was studying the building intently. And then he glanced at Wade, who was wearing a resigned expression that seemed to indicate he knew he was either going to have to stay out of the way or arrest someone. Namely Lucas.

Lucas had seen that look before—usually just before Chief Packer had hauled him off the jail.

Without another word to his brother-in-law-to-be, Lucas turned and kicked in the side door to the garage.

He heard Wade's curse, but he didn't wait around to discuss the finer points of trespassing. He entered the building, snapping on the overhead light as he entered.

Three covered vehicles sat inside the garage. A stack of cardboard boxes were piled against one wall. An interior door was set into the back wall. Lucas tested that one, finding it locked.

There was no one inside the garage, no sign that Rachel had ever been there.

Nosing around, Blake pulled the cover off the vehicle nearest him, revealing a 1950s-era pickup truck. Moving slowly, as if he knew better but couldn't resist, Wade uncovered the second vehicle, which turned out to be an orange two-seater. From where Lucas stood, he could see that the glove box hung open, and a pair of sunglasses lay on the passenger seat.

Turning to the third vehicle, Lucas took hold of the cover. He snapped it off with a flick of his wrist.

He stared at the vehicle he'd revealed, feeling as though someone had just hit him in the gut with a sledgehammer.

"Rachel's?" Blake murmured.

Unable, for the moment, to speak, Lucas nodded, then looked at Wade. Why would Rachel's car be hidden in Sam Jennings's garage? And where was she? If anything had happened to her…

Just the thought of losing her devastated him.

A quick, muffled sound from behind the door at the back of the garage made him go still.

A moment later, he lifted his booted foot again and slammed it against the locked door. The lock broke with a loud crack, and the door flew inward. Someone tried to rush past Lucas. He reached out and caught the guy with one hand, slamming him up against the garage wall.

"Get the hell off my property," Sam Jennings shouted, his florid face beet-red with fury and exertion. "Davenport, get this man away from me or be prepared to lose your badge."

Lucas gathered Sam's jacket in both hands and lifted him higher against the wall. "Tell me where Rachel is."

"I don't know what you're…"

"That's her car!" Lucas shouted into the man's face. "Where is she?"

"Davenport!" Sam's voice was strangled as he clawed at Lucas's hands. "Call him off."

"Damn it, Lucas." Wade yanked at Lucas's arm. "Let him go. I'll question him."

Lucas's voice was cold and controlled when he spoke. "If he's hurt Rachel, I'll kill him."

"Davenport!" Sam roared.

Lucas slammed the sweating man against the wall again. "God damn it, Jennings, where is she?"

"Could be you've caused her death, just as you did her brother's," Jennings snarled. There was pure hatred in his eyes as he glared up at the man who loomed so threateningly over him.

"I had nothing to do with Roger's death," Lucas answered, tightening his grip.

Jennings's voice was thin from lack of oxygen when he replied, refusing to surrender. "It was because of you that he was snooping around into the past, into things that didn't concern him. Because of you that Rachel was doing the same thing. You might as well have killed them both."

"Lucas, he's turning blue." Wade pushed again against Lucas's shoulders, trying to break his grip on the other man. "Let him go, or I'm going to have to arrest you."

"If he's done anything to Rachel, you're going to have to shoot me to keep me from killing him." Lucas's voice was cold. Flat. Utterly sincere.

"Lucas." Blake was still standing by Rachel's car. "I think I heard something. From the trunk..."

Lucas almost threw Jennings at Wade, who staggered, but caught Sam, restraining him when he tried to break away.

The car trunk was locked, of course.

"Where's the key, Jennings?" Lucas threw over his shoulder.

Jennings growled an obscenity, struggling futilely as Wade quickly and efficiently cuffed him. "Get them off my property, Davenport. You haven't got a warrant. You've got no cause to search my place."

Blake looked across the locked trunk to Lucas. "We can get into the trunk by taking out the back seat."

The doors to the vehicle were locked, as well.

Wade had already patted Jennings down. "No keys in his pockets," he reported.

Lucas looked around for something to break out the window. He found a tire iron in the storage space behind the seat of the orange sports car. A moment later, the sound of shattering glass echoed in the garage.

Lucas unlocked both back doors of Rachel's car, allowing him and Blake to lean in and start tugging at the loops built into the top of the back bench seat. It was the kind that folded down to extend the trunk space, allowing long items such as golf clubs to be hauled in the car. The seat opened to reveal a body crammed tightly in a fetal position in the narrow trunk space.

Lucas's heart nearly stopped. Rachel wasn't moving. At that moment, he felt his world crash in pieces around him.

He knew then that there would be no going on without her. Not this time.

Blake was already reaching in to ease Rachel out of the narrow space. Forcing himself out of his sick paralysis, Lucas helped him.

Her low, muffled moan was the most beautiful sound he'd ever heard.

She was alive.

Very carefully, he and Blake pulled her out of the car and laid her on the garage floor. Her hands and feet were strapped tightly together with duct tape, preventing her from moving, and another strip of the heavy gray tape covered her mouth. Her eyes were huge, her expression one of shock. The ugly bruise on one side of her face gave evidence that she hadn't gone into the trunk willingly.

Lucas and Blake knelt beside her. Lucas heard Wade talking to Sam Jennings, who'd gone very still and quiet, obviously realizing that he wouldn't be able to get away unscathed now.

"Are you all right?" Lucas asked, looking deeply into Rachel's dark, stunned eyes.

She nodded, a tear trickling down her right cheek.

"Let me get this off you, sweetheart," Blake murmured, taking hold of one corner of the tape across her mouth. "I'll be as gentle as I can."

Satisfied now that Rachel was safe, Lucas started to rise. "Take care of her, Blake. I want to have a talk with her uncle."

His fists itched to make Jennings pay for that bruise on Rachel's face. For the fear in her eyes.

Reading his intentions in his face, Rachel made a muffled sound of distress, reaching for him with her bound hands.

He hesitated, his gaze locked with her pleading one. And then he sighed and took her hands in his. "All right. We'll let the law take care of him," he muttered reluctantly. "Let's get rid of this tape."

"Thank you," she whispered as soon as Blake had freed her mouth.

Lucas cupped a hand behind her head and kissed her, mindful of the raw, bruised skin around her mouth, utterly heedless of his audience.

12

LUCAS WAS SITTING in his kitchen drinking coffee at five o'clock the next morning. He was trying to be quiet, since Emily, Wade, and Clay were all still sleeping. Lucas hadn't slept more than an hour all night.

He'd been so badly shaken by how close he'd come to losing Rachel that he was just now breathing normally again.

He loved her now as deeply as he had fifteen years ago—more, since he loved now with the intensity and complexity of a man's heart, not a boy's. And he knew that the man's heart was every bit as vulnerable as the boy's had been.

Things were far from settled between them, he thought, sipping his cooling coffee. There were plenty of strikes still against them. Local gossip would fly fast and furious once word got out of Sam Jennings's arrest. Would Rachel's mother unfairly blame Lucas for striking the final blow to the Jennings family?

At least Lucas hadn't killed Rachel's uncle—and he was uncomfortably aware of what a close call that had been.

He knew Rachel was a grown woman, that she'd been making her own decisions for a long time, but was she really ready to choose him over her only remaining family? Especially when they had been reunited for just less than a week, and a traumatic week at that.

Everything had happened so fast. So intensely. He didn't want her decisions influenced by volatile emotions—especially gratitude. If she said she loved him now, only to change her mind when she'd had more time to think about what she was doing—well, he didn't know if he could say good-bye to her again.

He had to give her time. He had to know, this time, that things wouldn't end badly. He had to be sure.

RACHEL WAS WELL AWARE of just how closely disaster had been averted Saturday evening. She didn't want to think about what her uncle might have done to her, had Lucas and the others not found her in time. And she didn't want to think what Lucas might have done to her uncle, had she not managed to calm him down.

Lucas McBride still had a fiery temper, she realized. He'd learned to control it, but it still simmered in that rebel heart of his. She knew without a doubt that he would never turn that temper against her. But he would always be willing to fight for the people he cared about.

She had known fifteen years ago that she had fallen in love with a dangerous man.

After all that time, some things hadn't changed.

By noon on Sunday, the gossips of Honoria were having a field day. A steady stream of visitors came by Rachel's grandmother's house on the pretext of offering sympathy and support, when many of them just wanted the juicy details of the latest McBride-Jennings scandal. Though the truth was bizarre enough, it was still embroidered in the re-telling Rachel heard. Rumor had it that guns had been drawn. Shots fired. Bodies found. That Chief Davenport and Tara McBride's dashing P.I. husband had barely prevented Lucas from killing Sam Jennings.

With startling small-town fickleness, some people had transformed Lucas from a shadowy murderer suspect into a bold, bad-boy hero who had come home to protect his sister and had daringly saved Rachel's life. And it didn't hurt his standing in the community that word had leaked out about the sizeable fortune he'd made with his own computer company. Wealth and success had an amazing way of polishing a tarnished reputation.

Some correct information was also distributed. Sam Jennings had been arrested for assault and battery and the subsequent imprisonment of his niece. He was being questioned in connection with the break-in and assault on Emily McBride several months earlier. There were also questions about whether he'd been involved in the disappearance twenty-four years earlier of his brother Al and Al's lover, Nadine Peck McBride. It was even possible, some whispered, that Sam had pushed his nephew to his death.

Rachel's grandmother had been so upset that she spent most of Sunday in bed, recuperating. Rachel's mother, Jane, became completely hysterical when Rachel tried over the telephone to discuss what had happened. She sounded almost as disturbed by the news that Lucas McBride had rescued Rachel as by everything that Sam had done.

"So she would rather have had you die in that car trunk than to have me be the one to find you there?" Lucas asked when he called just after her difficult conversation with her mother Sunday afternoon.

"No, not quite that bad. Mother just didn't know you and I were dating before Roger died and it was a shock for her to find out we've been seeing each other again while I've been back in town. Don't forget, for the past fifteen years she's considered you a suspect in her son's death—thanks, in part, to Sam's blaming you so adamantly," she added bitterly.

She and Lucas hadn't had much chance to talk after he'd pulled her out of her car. Dazed from the shock of everything that had happened to her—as well as from the blow that had rendered her unconscious long enough for Sam to bind her and stuff her into her trunk—she hardly remembered anything that had happened after the rescue. Lucas had insisted on taking her to the emergency room of the nearest hospital, where she'd been examined and released, and then he'd brought her to her distraught grandmother, where he'd left her to rest. She knew he'd gone straight to the police department when he left her, wanting to know exactly what penalties Sam would pay.

"Has my uncle talked?" she asked Lucas, clutching the receiver in a hand that was suddenly unsteady.

"Not much," Lucas replied, his voice grim. "Wade can't even get him to admit now that he stuffed you into your car trunk—though, of course, he won't get away with that one."

"No, he won't," Rachel agreed, her voice hard. "Was any other evidence found to connect him with my father? Or with Roger?"

"Wade found some letters Sam had stashed away. Several were from Nadine—steamy love letters, a few containing hints for gifts or money. Some were written before her marriage to my father…and the rest were written afterward."

Rachel gasped. "Nadine was seeing both my uncle *and* my father after her marriage?"

"Apparently." Lucas sounded utterly disgusted with his stepmother's behavior. "Sounds as if she was playing them all for fools. And it's pretty obvious that Sam, for one, was obsessed with her."

"Do you think Roger found out?"

"Wade also found a letter Roger wrote to Sam a few days before he died telling him the same theory Roger had given me—that my father was a murderer. In the letter, he told Sam he'd found the bracelet and Al's wallet and that he was going to be spending a lot of time looking for more evidence. He said he wanted it in writing in case anything happened to him—he apparently thought either my father or I would be a threat to him."

"Where was the letter found?" Rachel asked, stunned by the implications. "Why on earth wouldn't Sam have destroyed it?"

"It was in small safe hidden in one of Sam's closets. Apparently, Sam thought it might be useful against the McBrides someday. Remember, it implicated my father, not Sam."

"But my father's car was in his garage."

"He told Wade Al gave it to him before he left."

"I don't believe that."

"Neither do I. Not considering everything else we've found. The bracelet is going to be hard for him to brush off. Wade recognized it immediately, as you did. Emily will identify it as the one she was wearing when she was attacked." Lucas paused. "Wade and I looked very closely at that bracelet last night, after I took you home. There was something about it none of us had noticed before."

"What?"

"That heavy oval clasp—it had a hidden latch. When pressed, the clasp opened. Like a locket. Since Emily had only worn it a few weeks before it was stolen from her, she'd never discovered the mechanism."

Rachel held her breath as she asked, "What was inside?"

"An engraved inscription. Faint, but still readable under a magnifying glass. 'To N. from S. Mine forever.'"

"Mine forever," Rachel whispered. "It makes jealousy sound more than ever like a motive, doesn't it?"

"Could be that he managed to deal with her leaving him for Josiah. But finding out that she was having an affair with his own brother sent him over the edge."

"Lucas—" Rachel moistened her lips. "Do you think we'll ever know for certain what happened to my father and your stepmother?"

"I don't know. Maybe Sam will eventually talk. He's hardly stable—and everything that happened yesterday has shaken him badly."

"He didn't want to kill me. The only thing he said to me before he hit me was that he was tired of hurting his family."

"He's almost destroyed his family," Lucas answered grimly.

Rachel had to agree. If everything they'd come to believe about Sam was true, he'd murdered his own brother and nephew, had caused his sister-in-law to become a neurotic mess, and had almost killed his niece. If it had been Sam's intention to ruin the McBrides, he had failed. The McBrides were thriving. The Jennings family was broken.

"I'm sorry, Rachel," Lucas said, as if he'd followed her thoughts. "You didn't deserve any of this."

"And you didn't deserve to be labeled a murderer," she replied. "Sam has caused so much pain for both our families. He should pay."

"One way or another, he will."

"Lucas—" She frowned, not trusting his tone. "Promise me you'll stay away from him. Whatever happens with the legal system, swear to me you won't try to take the law into your own hands."

"He almost killed you." The barely suppressed fury sizzled through the telephone line, almost burning Rachel's fingers.

"Promise me, Lucas," she said steadily. Firmly.

He grumbled. "I'll leave him alone. Unless he ever bothers you or my sister again. And then all promises are off."

"Thank you. That's as much as I can expect, I suppose," she said wryly.

It was sort of like being in love with a Doberman pinscher, she reflected. He was utterly loyal to those he protected, but beware to anyone who threatened them.

"You're doing okay? You aren't having any problems from the blow to your head?"

She shook off the image and replied, "No, I'm fine. Will I see you tonight?"

There was a pause. And then, "You should probably get some rest this evening. And I'm sure your grandmother needs you."

Rachel began to frown. Something in Lucas's voice put her on alert. "And what will *you* be doing this evening?"

"I'll have dinner with Emily, Wade and Clay— and then I thought I'd head back to California. There's a flight leaving Atlanta at midnight. All I have to do is turn in the rental car and…"

"You're leaving?" Rachel interrupted in disbelief. *"Tonight?"*

"Emily has a lot to do during the next week. She's getting married Friday evening. She doesn't need me underfoot."

"You know very well that Emily wants you at her wedding and that she does not see you as a burden in any way. Why are you leaving, Lucas?"

"It just seems best. Everyone in town is talking about the McBrides again. I don't want to turn the wedding into a circus."

"I don't believe that. What are you running from this time, Lucas?" She didn't even try to keep the anger out of her voice.

"I'm not running. I said all along that I would only stay through Christmas, and that's what I've done. I also promised I wouldn't leave this time without saying goodbye."

"So that's why you called? To say goodbye?"

"And to make sure you're all right."

"How very kind of you."

Her sarcasm must have hit home, but he went on as if he hadn't heard her. "I'm leaving my address and telephone number with Wade and Emily. Wade will bring them by to you, if you're interested."

"Mmm." She was so angry she felt as if she could snap the telephone receiver in half.

"You'll know where I'll be, if you ever want to talk, or visit California—or whatever," he finished, sounding uncharacteristically awkward. "This doesn't have to be a permanent goodbye—unless you want it to be."

She didn't reply.

"Rachel?"

"You, Lucas McBride, are a coward," she informed him coolly. And then she slammed down the receiver.

She had almost forgotten in her fanciful imagining earlier that ferocious guard dogs sometimes turned unexpectedly against the people they were supposed to protect.

AN HOUR LATER, Lucas still felt as if his ear was ringing from that crashing disconnection. Rachel had been furious with him—that was easy enough to figure out. What he couldn't quite understand was what she had really expected.

He stood alone in the rock house, leaning against a wall and staring morosely out the window opening that faced the bluffs, contemplating Rachel's reactions.

It wasn't as if he'd disappeared without a word again. After all that had passed between them, he could understand why that would make her angry. But he'd called to tell her his plans, and even offered his address and phone number. What more did she want from him?

It seemed he was about to find out.

"Hiding, Lucas?"

Frowning, he turned to find Rachel standing in the doorway, her hands on her hips, her brows drawn into a frown. "How did you know I would be here?"

"I didn't. I went to Emily's house first. When she said you'd taken a walk before dinner, I knew where to find you."

Her face was still pale, he noted in concern. The bruise at her temple looked dark and painful against her skin. The sight of it brought back the murderous rage he'd felt when he'd found her in the trunk of her car yesterday. If Sam Jennings had been within reach, Lucas couldn't have guaranteed that he would keep his promise to Rachel not to smash the bastard's face in.

He'd thought it would be easier to leave if he didn't see her again. Otherwise, he might not be able to give her the time he believed she needed before she made any major decisions. Looking at her now—so pale, and yet so beautiful, so vulnerable, and yet so ferocious—all he wanted to do was take her in his arms and never let her go.

He'd been right to try to stay away from her.

"Why did you come?" he asked, pushing his hands into the pockets of his leather jacket to keep himself from reaching for her.

"I have a few things to say. And I want to be looking at you when I say them."

"Rachel..."

She dropped her hands from her hips and stepped toward him. "Do you know what you did to me fifteen years ago? You broke my heart. No, you didn't just break it. You shattered it."

"I told you, Rachel. I didn't sleep with Lizzie. I didn't..."

"Yes, you told me. Fifteen years later. Why didn't you tell me *then?*"

"You wouldn't talk to me."

"You called me one time, nearly two months after my brother died—during an evening when my mother and grandmother were there to hear every word I might have said to you. If you had really wanted to talk to me, you would have made more than that token gesture."

He was beginning to feel defensive. He drew his jacket more closely around him. "You knew where to contact me, if you'd wanted to."

"For all I knew, you were spending all your time with Lizzie! How was I to know differently?"

"You could have *trusted* me," he snapped back. "For all I knew, you thought I had killed your brother."

"So why didn't you tell me you didn't?"

"I shouldn't have had to tell you. You should have known me better."

"As it happens, I did," she answered quietly. "I never for one moment thought you had anything to do with Roger's death."

She'd told him that before. He wasn't sure he'd fully believed it—until now.

"Rachel…"

She jabbed a finger into his chest. Painfully. "You ran. You decided I'd judged you, just like the rest of the town, and instead of staying to convince me differently, you took off. You asked me to *marry* you, Lucas! And I said yes. I asked if we could wait until I finished college, and you said that wasn't a problem, that you needed time to find a better job than that one you had then. You said you would wait. But you left."

Her finger was nearly digging a hole in his chest. Lucas reached up to catch her hand, holding it firmly, but carefully.

"I was doing you a favor, damn it. Even if you didn't think I was a killer, the rest of your family sure as hell did. More than half the town did. We couldn't have kept seeing each other without someone else finding out. I couldn't stay here with everyone believing what they did about me, my father refusing to have anything to do with me, my sister being penalized just for being related to me. I *had* to leave. I couldn't take you with me, even if you'd wanted to go. I had no job, no home, nothing. You were too young to be put into that position. You deserved more."

He wasn't in a habit of explaining himself in so much detail. His associates in California had learned not to ask questions, just to accept whatever he chose to share with them.

Rachel wasn't going to be so easily satisfied.

She jerked her hand away from his and jabbed him with her finger again. "And what are you protecting me from *this* time?"

"Everything happened so fast this past week. I

was giving you time to think. Time to decide if you want this to go any farther. I was leaving you my number," he reminded her.

"In other words, you decided again what was best for me, just as you did fifteen years ago. Well, let me tell you, Lucas McBride, I didn't need you making decisions for me then, and I certainly don't now."

"I…"

She gave him no chance to speak. "If you want to leave because you aren't interested in a serious relationship with me, then go. I survived before, I will again. But I don't think that's what you want at all. I think you want to be with me. I think you want to be here to see your sister married. I think you're just too damned scared of real, honest, overwhelming emotion. I think you've stopped believing in lifetime commitment, because it's not something you've experienced before. Your mother died, your stepmother ran off, your father withdrew, the town turned against you…and I hung up on you. And those hurts have left you an emotional coward."

"Rachel…" His voice was husky. He felt as if he were bleeding from a dozen small wounds, all inflicted by words that rang painfully true.

"I'm sorry for hurting you, Lucas. I'm sorry I was too young and naive and overwhelmed by events to trust you as I should have. You hurt me, too, but I've gotten past it. I'm ready to go on from here. But this time, you're going to have to take a risk. You're going to have to tell me how you feel and what you want. You're going to have to swallow some of that McBride stubbornness and pride and..."

As fascinating as he'd found her tirade, as beautiful as she looked with fire in her dark eyes and a flush of determination on her face, he knew it was his turn to speak. "I love you, Rachel."

She closed her mouth and stared at him narrowly. "What did you say?"

"I love you. I have since I was a stupid, hot-tempered kid. I've never stopped. *Never.*"

It was as close to baring his soul as Lucas knew how to do.

She closed her eyes for a moment, as if in relief. He noticed her hand was trembling when she reached beneath her collar and drew out a thin gold chain. A gold heart-shaped charm dangled from her hand. "You made me a promise when you gave me this," she said. "Do you remember what it was?"

The sight of the charm made him swallow hard. Oh, yes, he remembered giving it to her. He remembered the look on her face when she'd opened it. The love in her eyes.

If he'd known Lizzie had been going around saying he'd given *her* one, too, he'd have...

But he couldn't think about what he should have done. Or start second-guessing the choices he had made. He could drive himself crazy that way. "I remember."

"You said we would be married when I finished college and you had a secure income from a stable job. Well, I finished college eleven years ago. And rumor has it you've got a good job. Are you a man who reneges on his promises, Lucas McBride?'' she challenged him, her cheeks flushed, her gaze level.

Something tight and painful eased inside him. He was still a bit worried that things were happening too fast, that Rachel would change her mind once she'd had time to think—but he would be the world's biggest fool to walk away from her again when she had done everything but order him to stay. Her courage humbled him—and showed him how right she'd been when she'd called him an emotional coward.

''Not anymore,'' he answered her, holding out his arms.

She walked into them, wrapping her own tightly around him. ''I love you, Lucas. I loved you when I was eighteen, and I've fallen in love with you all over again at thirty-three.''

He held her tightly, his face buried in her hair. ''Your family is going to hate this. Your mother…''

''Will have to get used to it,'' she broke in firmly. ''This is my choice, not hers.''

''We can take it slow, if you want,'' he felt compelled to say, giving her one last out. ''Give you time to make absolutely sure…''

''Lucas.'' She looked up at him, her mouth inches from his. ''Do *you* need more time?''

''Hell, no,'' he muttered, his tone heartfelt. ''If it was up to me, I'd marry you right now. Right here. Never let you out of my sight again. But…''

''Then shut up and kiss me,'' she murmured, reaching up to tug his head down to hers.

He smiled ruefully against her lips. ''You've become a bossy woman, Rachel Jennings.'' He wasn't complaining.

"Yes. I figure I have to be to keep up with you."

"You could be right," he conceded. And then he allowed himself to kiss her, knowing he would be lost when he did.

He was right. The first brush of her lips against his made his head spin. And when she moved closer to him, bringing their bodies in full contact through their bulky winter clothing, he lost all remnants of self-control.

Crushing her mouth beneath his, he twisted, holding her against the hard rock wall. He reached between them, fumbling with her jacket, and with the buttons of the heavy brushed-cotton shirt she wore beneath it. He spread the garments open, baring her skin to his searching hands. Savoring her softness, he slid his palms up her sides and cupped her breasts through the lace of her bra.

Rachel groaned into his mouth, her hips pressing into his, against the erection that strained against his zipper. After spending the morning trying to be noble, telling himself there was a chance he wouldn't see her again, the sheer relief of having her with him now went straight to his heart—and to his groin. He wanted her as he couldn't remember ever wanting before.

Rachel's hands were busy, pushing his leather jacket aside, fumbling with the buttons of his denim shirt. She crowded against him, and her skin felt warm against his. He tugged her bra out of the way, flattening her soft, firm breasts against his chest.

They moaned in unison.

Snaps were unfastened, zippers lowered. Lucas reached inside her jeans and cupped her bottom, lifting her against him. Their breathing was ragged, their movements frantic. Rachel wrapped her arms around his neck, clinging tightly.

For one brief, lucid moment, Lucas became aware of their surroundings. The chill in the air. The roughness of the rock behind Rachel's back. "You can't be comfortable," he murmured, lowering her tenderly to her feet. Trying so damned hard to rein in his hunger. "We should wait. Find a bed…"

"Next time," she whispered, moving sinuously against him. "I want you, Lucas. Love me."

She reached down to take him in her hand. His knees almost buckled. Next time, he told himself as he lifted her against the wall again, he would give her romance. Flowers, candlelight, a soft bed. This time he could only give her himself.

Rachel seemed to have no complaints when he thrust deeply, heavily into her. Her soft, choked cry sounded pleased, excited—and maybe a little triumphant.

Lucas knew in that moment that he had finally come home.

Epilogue

LUCAS TUGGED restlessly at the too-tight collar of his tuxedo. "I think I'm choking."

"When's the last time you wore a tie?" Emily asked, smiling up at him from within the layers of white net that framed her face.

"I haven't the faintest idea," he answered candidly.

"Well, you look great. So stop complaining and try to enjoy it."

Enjoy it? Not likely. Lucas's stomach was knotted as he and Emily waited in the church vestibule for their cue to enter. Wade and his best man, proud-looking Clay, and a groomsman who was one of Wade's deputies, waited at the altar. The bridesmaids—Savannah and Tara—had just gone in, and it would be Lucas and Emily's turn any minute now.

How did he let himself get talked into staying for this wedding, anyway—not to mention giving the bride away? But even as the question crossed his mind, he knew the answer. Rachel and Emily had joined forces; Lucas hadn't stood a chance against them.

With a sinking feeling, he heard the bridal march begin, signaling that it was time. He drew a deep breath, hoping everything would go well. This was his sister's wedding day. He would hate for anything to spoil it—especially anything having to do with him.

"I love you, Lucas," Emily said, smiling up at him with stars in her beautiful blue eyes.

He bent his head to kiss her cheek. "I love you, too, little sister. Now, let's go get you married."

He shouldn't have worried. Emily was so radiantly beautiful in her wedding finery that all eyes turned immediately to her when he walked with her into the church. He knew there were those who were eagerly watching him, as well. But the gawking wasn't nearly as bad as he'd expected.

He delivered Emily safely to her groom, then, with a sigh of relief, took his seat on the pew beside Rachel.

She reached out to take his hand, probably fueling the gossip that would surely follow the wedding. Lucas didn't care. He squeezed her fingers, anticipating his own upcoming wedding. He and Rachel would be married quietly, with only their families around them. Her mother would be there, as well—dressed in black, perhaps, he thought wryly, but there.

Now that Sam Jennings had finally confessed to everything—the murders of Al and Nadine, as well as the death of his nephew, Roger—which, he continued to insist, had been an accident and ultimately Lucas's fault—and the break-in at Emily's house, Jane had conceded that Lucas was innocent and had daringly saved her daughter's life. She didn't have to like it that Rachel planned to marry a McBride, but she wasn't going to cause trouble.

Lucas would be taking his bride to California,

where her expertise with business accounting would be a valuable asset to Rebel Software.

"Now," Rachel whispered. "Aren't you glad you stayed?"

He looked at the altar, where Emily and Wade repeated their vows while Clay stood beaming at his father's side and newlyweds Savannah and Tara looked on in misty-eyed approval. And then he looked at Rachel, who smiled at him with such acceptance and contentment that his heart swelled.

"Yeah," he muttered. "I'm very glad I stayed."

Oblivious to the onlookers, and no longer concerned with the gossip, Lucas leaned over to kiss Rachel. Their lips met at the same time his little sister kissed her new husband at the front of the church.

The scandalous McBrides had found everything they'd been looking for, right here in their little hometown.

It's hotter than a winter fire.
It's a BLAZE!

In January 1999 stay warm with another
one of our bold, provocative, *ultra-sexy*
Temptation novels.

#715 *TANTALIZING*
by Lori Foster

It was lust at first sight—but Josie and Mark were both
pretending to be other people! They were giving new
meaning to the term "blind date." How to unravel the web
of deceit? And still hang on to that sexy stranger…

BLAZE!
Red-hot reads from Temptation!

Available wherever Harlequin books are sold.

Take 2 bestselling love stories FREE

Plus get a FREE surprise gift!

Special Limited-Time Offer

Mail to Harlequin Reader Service®

3010 Walden Avenue
P.O. Box 1867
Buffalo, N.Y. 14240-1867

YES! Please send me 2 free Harlequin Temptation® novels and my free surprise gift. Then send me 4 brand-new novels every month, which I will receive before they appear in bookstores. Bill me at the low price of $3.12 each plus 25¢ delivery and applicable sales tax, if any.* That's the complete price, and a saving of over 10% off the cover prices—quite a bargain! I understand that accepting the books and gift places me under no obligation ever to buy any books. I can always return a shipment and cancel at any time. Even if I never buy another book from Harlequin, the 2 free books and the surprise gift are mine to keep forever.

142 HEN CH7G

Name	(PLEASE PRINT)	
Address		Apt. No.
City	State	Zip

This offer is limited to one order per household and not valid to present Harlequin Temptation® subscribers. *Terms and prices are subject to change without notice. Sales tax applicable in N.Y.

UTEMP-98   ©1990 Harlequin Enterprises Limited

HARLEQUIN Temptation®

He's strong. He's sexy.
He's up for grabs!

Harlequin Temptation and
Texas Men magazine present:

1998 Mail Order Men

Mail Order Men—
Satisfaction Guaranteed!

Available wherever Harlequin books are sold.

HARLEQUIN®
Makes any time special ™

Look us up on-line at: http://www.romance.net

HTEMOM

***For a limited time, Harlequin and Silhouette
have an offer you just can't refuse.***

In November and December 1998:

BUY **ANY** TWO HARLEQUIN
OR SILHOUETTE BOOKS and
SAVE $10.00
off future purchases

OR BUY ANY THREE HARLEQUIN OR SILHOUETTE BOOKS
AND **SAVE $20.00** OFF FUTURE PURCHASES!

(each coupon is good for $1.00 off the purchase of two
Harlequin or Silhouette books)

....

JUST BUY 2 HARLEQUIN OR SILHOUETTE BOOKS, SEND US YOUR
NAME, ADDRESS AND 2 PROOFS OF PURCHASE (CASH REGISTER
RECEIPTS) AND HARLEQUIN WILL SEND YOU A COUPON BOOKLET
WORTH **$10.00 OFF** FUTURE PURCHASES OF HARLEQUIN OR
SILHOUETTE BOOKS IN 1999. SEND US 3 PROOFS OF PURCHASE AND
WE WILL SEND YOU 2 COUPON BOOKLETS WITH A TOTAL SAVING OF
$20.00. (ALLOW 4-6 WEEKS DELIVERY) OFFER EXPIRES
DECEMBER 31, 1998.

....

I accept your offer! Please send me a coupon booklet(s), to:

NAME: _____

ADDRESS: _____

CITY: _____ STATE/PROV.: _____ POSTAL/ZIP CODE: _____

Send your name and address, along with your cash register
receipts for proofs of purchase, to:

In the U.S.	In Canada
Harlequin Books	**Harlequin Books**
P.O. Box 9057	**P.O. Box 622**
Buffalo, NY	**Fort Erie, Ontario**
14269	**L2A 5X3**